ONE WHO KNOWS
HORSES

Max Windham

authorHOUSE®

AuthorHouse™ UK
1663 Liberty Drive
Bloomington, IN 47403 USA
www.authorhouse.co.uk
Phone: 0800.197.4150

Published by AuthorHouse 10/14/2017

ISBN: 978-1-5462-8334-8 (sc)
ISBN: 978-1-5462-8335-5 (hc)
ISBN: 978-1-5462-8346-1 (e)

Library of Congress Control Number: 2017915706

Print information available on the last page.

CHAPTER ONE

The year was 1830, and I, Zachery Morris, had left the hot humidity of Mississippi with my big stallion, Ollie, named after a dead cousin I'd grown up with. Ollie was my closest friend. We had been together since the day Ollie was born.

We now were looking at the Rocky Mountains with the four companions I had met in St. Louis. Mathew Sparks was the leader, and the others included an old trapper named Pete Hayden and a set of twins. Mathew had painted a pretty picture of the mountains and the riches to be made. Mathew was about forty years old and talked as if he knew all about trapping. Pete Hayden seemed to be around just to make Mathew's life easy. He seemed to need Mathew to handle the thinking part, because he did nothing until Mathew gave him orders. Pete made Mathew's bed for him, and when they made camp, he cooked. He brought the food to Mathew and then washed his plate. The rest of the time, he stayed quiet and would find a spot out of people's way. He could squat down and sit there until Mathew called, and then he would pop up and hurry to Mathew. The twins were identical, and none of us knew their real names. We would just call, "Twin!" and one or the other would answer. I never knew why they would not give their names, and I assumed they were running from the law. In the beginning, they acted friendly enough. They were excited to have a job and a chance to make big money.

So far, the picture of the mountains that Mathew had painted was correct. To stand before them and look at their beauty was worth the trip. I was looking from the south to the north as far as I could see. Mathew had said that he could not do these mountains justice—that you had to stand before them. I could only imagine how far they extended in each direction.

I thought of the distance I had traveled after leaving home. I knew that it was just a minor distance compared to the length of this mountain range. They were snow-capped, with jagged ridges. Timber grew up to the snow line. We had seen them the day before. They looked like clouds rising with the snow on top. Now we were here, and it was time to start climbing higher. To find the beaver streams, we would have to travel over passes that no white man had traveled. We would go into valleys where the beaver had made ponds for generations. There would be Indians whom we would have to always be on the alert for—or lose our hair—and wild animals, such as the grizzly bear. The dangers were here, but if we were successful, we would have more money than an eighteen-year-old boy could imagine. Soon I would be a part of this new world. I would have preferred making this trip with my cousin and childhood friend, but that was no longer possible.

I had noticed after leaving St. Louis a change in my four companions. They had asked more than once to buy Ollie. At times without my permission, they had tried to saddle him. Ollie had not been around anyone but me and did not allow anyone to handle him. It was as if he could detect the evil in men. The farther west we traveled, the heavier my workload became. It was beginning to look like I was the low man on the totem pole.

On one occasion, Twin said that, if he had that horse, he would break him and teach him some manners. One way or another, Ollie was always being worked into the conversation.

Ollie was not a horse that you broke. His mother had died soon after his birth, and I had raised him from day one. As we had traveled, men had seen this stallion as a bloodline they would love to own. They had wanted to use him to breed their mares, but Ollie and I had other plans.

We made camp our first night after entering the mountains. We had gained altitude that first day and stopped early to let the horses adjust to the thinner air. I staked Ollie and my two pack horses away from the others. The men's attitude had changed toward me after they'd come to understand that Ollie would never be for sale. As we'd crossed the plains, I'd started making plans to get away. Traveling alone would be much more dangerous. But if things continued like they were, staying with my partners could be just as dangerous. I had hoped to get away before entering the mountains. We were here now, and I had to get away while I could use Ollie's speed and endurance on the open plains.

Twin must have had a bad day and felt it was his duty to show his ignorance. "You'd better put that horse farther away. If he kicks at me again, I will blow his brains all over these mountains."

Now I had my excuse. I would move him farther out from the rest. Maybe I would be able to leave without my absence being detected till morning. I could sneak out at night and get enough of a head start. I felt that I could at least get away without being noticed.

I had held my temper in check during the trip. I did not know whether any of my companions would be of help to me if one or more of the others jumped me. But more and more, I felt alone. Mathew, being our leader, had not said anything on the issue of my horse. He had stayed away from it like it was not any of his business. Instead of working together to form a team, each of the four men I was with seemed to have an idea of his own.

I moved Ollie and my two pack horses far enough away and spoke loudly enough that everyone could hear. "If you get kicked now, it will be your fault. You have no reason to be close to him."

When I made my move, I would not be able to make a sound. It did not take much to wake any of us. After we had had our meal, the others were getting ready for bed. While I was rubbing my horses down, I overheard Twin.

"It won't be long before I own that horse."

Mathew said, "Don't go jumping the gun. I had designs on that horse all along. Why do you think I let him tag along?"

I knew then that I needed to leave as soon as possible. We were not so far into the mountains that I couldn't be back on the plains within an hour. There would be no way they could catch up with Ollie once he stretched those long legs. He would be able to run all night and part of the next day. I might have to leave my packhorses to outrun them. I could always get more pack horses if they could not keep up, but so far, they had trailed Ollie with no problems. Right now, I was worried about stopping a bullet with my back.

I had brought a couple of bottles of whiskey for medicine. My mother and father had always mixed whiskey and honey and had given it to me for any ailment I had. I got one of the bottles and walked back to the fire, pulled the cork, and took a big swallow. Twin was the first to jump up and reach for the bottle. Somehow he thought that my property was the same as his property.

"You have been holding out on the rest of us. I ought to blow your brains out. Why didn't you tell us that you had this all along?"

It was that kind of attitude that had gotten more aggressive each day. I handed the rest of the bottle to Mathew.

"Boys, I have been saving this for a special occasion. It was for the first night in the mountains. We are here now, so let's drink to a successful season."

The other twin asked, "What else have you hidden from us?"

"If you try to find out, you may realize that you have made a mistake you won't be able to correct." I can usually control my temper, and I had to now if this was to work. I would have to walk away before it got out of hand. I had already set the wheels in motion and could not chance anything upsetting my plans.

Twin started to reply, but Mathew spoke up. "Relax. Take a swallow of this before it's gone. We probably won't get any more before rendezvous."

With that, each tried to drink as big a portion as possible in case the bottle did not make it back around.

I started to reach for it. Twin grabbed it, saying, "You will be standing first watch, and you need to keep your eyes on those horses. We will save you a share. You won't need any until you go to bed. I will spell you in about two hours."

I kinda looked as if I had my doubts of ever seeing that bottle again. But in truth, I would be happy to let them consume the whole thing.

I went to their horses and spoke to them while rubbing them down. I made a big show of being the one taking proper care of the horses. I would allow the men to enjoy the bottle while I was getting the horses used to me stirring around. I needed those horses to make no sound after the rest had gone to sleep. They were talking loudly and already spending money they had not made. They had brought up the subject of the Indian women that they were going to buy. The whiskey was doing its job. The louder they talked, the drunker they were.

When the bottle was empty, they begin to settle down and go to sleep. I figured with that much whiskey in them they would not wake before sunrise. They started the snoring that had kept me awake many nights. I eased over to Ollie and the packhorses and began to load them. When I had them loaded and felt that the men were sleeping soundly, I moved the pack horses one at a time farther away to keep the noise down and came back for Ollie.

I got on Ollie and told him, "We only have one chance, so let's make it count."

We were out of camp about one hundred yards when I felt the bullet tear through my side. Someone must have woken to go to the bushes and saw me leaving. I grabbed the horn of the saddle and kicked Ollie and hung on. I knew that, if I could stay in the saddle, Ollie would get me out of this situation. But what situation would I wind up in? There were wild Indians out there, and I did not know where I was going. But this way I had a chance. I was alone now and riding a stallion that men were willing to kill me to get. I needed to stay in control, but the pain and loss of blood were beginning to take a toll. I wondered who had put the bullet in me. I would love to return it one day. But now I had to put some distance between us. They were probably in their saddles following me now.

We had traveled through the night, and Ollie had held a steady pace. Twice during the night, I had been aware that Ollie had stopped. I did not know if he was sensing which direction to go, or maybe he was only resting. Each time he had stopped, I had wanted to get off and stop the pain in my side. Sometime before daylight, I had fallen from his back. I remembered Ollie nuzzling me to get up. When I tried, darkness flooded my brain.

When I opened my eyes again, the sun was so bright I thought my head would explode. I knew that, somehow, I had to get up and keep moving. I did not know how long I had lay there, and my old partners could be getting close. If they caught up with me, my life would not be worth the empty bottle in camp. I had escaped from them with Ollie, and they would not be willing to let me get away. They had already said they had to have Ollie and proved that they were willing to kill me for him.

Horses like Ollie were one in a million. My father had bred his best brood mare to a fine stallion in New Orleans. We had no idea that the colt would turn out so good. I wished my father had lived to see Ollie.

Men like the four I had traveled with, where there was no law, took what they wanted even if they had to kill. Although I had shown no weakness, these were the kind of men to shoot you in the back and never think about it again. They knew the value of a horse like Ollie. When the Indians were after you, without speed and staying power such as Ollie had, your scalp might be used to decorate a warrior's spear.

After I was able to move again, I whistled, and Ollie come to me. I managed to stand by holding the stirrup. I had taught Ollie that, when I tapped him on the leg, he was to stretch out, allowing me to mount much easier. Ollie got down—it seemed like he understood that I was hurt—and stretched until his stomach almost touched the ground. The pain in my side was so bad that I had to grit my teeth to get mounted. I had to keep moving. With me on his back, Ollie got up and headed north at a smooth pace. The pain was intense, and I knew it would not be long before I would pass out again. If I could stay in the saddle, Ollie would do the rest. I could only hope the pack horses would follow.

During the time I was able to stay awake, Ollie changed course and headed into the mountains. When the first low branch almost dragged me from his back, I lay down on Ollie's neck to keep them from pulling me from my saddle. Ollie kept zigzagging farther into the mountains until he came to a small pool. He stopped, and as my feet touched the ground, I knew immediately my legs would not hold me. Again, the darkness flooded my brain.

CHAPTER TWO

I don't know how long I lay there. But as I was coming to, I was aware that Ollie was standing very close and not letting something or someone get close to me. When I was able to focus, I saw an Indian warrior and two young women. One looked to be in her twenties and the other about fifteen. The warrior seemed to be very old and was not acting hostile. He was not painted in war paint as I had heard they did, and I was not immediately frightened. It was more like they wanted Ollie to move away so they could check my wound.

I knew that I needed help, so I had to trust these people. My side was hurting, I had lost a lot of blood, and I was cold. I spoke to Ollie, calming him down. He backed away, but he kept both eyes on the old man. They wanted to come to me but did not know what this big stallion might do. The old Indian looked at Ollie; he had the same look I had seen so many times before. I knew his first thoughts were that he should steal this horse.

"Will it be okay to approach you now?" asked one of the women, using good English.

"As long as you mean me no harm. If you do, there is no telling what he might do."

Now I had no way of knowing that he would do anything. But the Indians knew that this horse had stood for me. They were not likely to test such a stallion as this.

The young girl spoke to the warrior, and he headed down the trail back tracking me. To the girl with her, she spoke and pointed in the woods. The girl left in that direction. This young woman was giving orders, and the other two were obeying. With her taking charge, I felt much better. She seemed too kind to have bad intentions.

"My name is Zack. Where did you learn to speak English?"

I was hoping maybe there were some white men close by that I might team up with. I had left what I knew was a bad situation, and although these people seemed to mean me no harm, I felt I needed to be around my own kind.

"My name is Spring Flower, the old warrior's name is Two Mountains, and the other girl's name is Night Dove."

She explained to me that, when she was a young girl, some white men had spent a winter in their camp. And they had a black man that traveled with them. When they left, Two Mountains had agreed to go with them as a guide to the big water where the sun set.

She asked, "Have you ever seen a black man before?"

"Where I came from, there were a few."

Two Mountains had learned the language, and she had learned from him. She explained to him that the white men had told them to be friendly when other white men came—that more white men would follow and they would need to know the white man's language. The white man would bring many things to trade for that would help them make life easier.

She had pulled the shirt off my body and was washing the wound. She was so gentle I hardly felt any pain. While we waited for Night Dove to return with the herbs, she made a bed from dry leaves and covered it with one of my blankets.

"Get the bottle of whiskey from my pack and pour it on my wounds. It will help me to heal and keep infection out."

I did not know what she knew of medicine or tending of gunshot wounds.

"The whiskey is not what you need. And do not let Two Mountains know you have whiskey. He would drink it all and go crazy. He got whiskey last year when he went to the rendezvous and came back with nothing. He had gotten drunk and wasted his furs. The whiskey brought by the white men caused our warriors to go crazy. When they have traded all their furs, our warriors will then trade their women to get more."

When Night Dove returned, Spring Flower took the herbs and rolled them in a ball and mashed them into a pulp. She then pressed the pulp into my wounds. She tore my shirt and wrapped it around my waist to protect the wound.

"This will kill the infection and break your fever."

While she worked, she asked me. "Do you have any food?"

With all my plans of my escape, I had only stored some jerky. I did not think that I would be able to stop and cook for a day or two. I had hoped that, after I escaped, I would be able to shoot what I would need.

"I only have some jerky. It's in my pack. You are welcome to it."

The two women quickly made camp, and we ate the jerked meat that I had in my bag. The two girls acted as if they had not eaten in days.

"The old man, Two Mountains, where did you send him?"

"I sent him back down the trail to keep watch—to see if the ones that shot you were following. He will watch the trail and will return in the morning. If anyone follows, he will let us know, and we can be ready for them. He is good at reading signs."

With darkness, they put me to bed. Each squaw got on one side of me, putting me in the middle. Spring Flower noticed me looking a mite uncomfortable.

She said, "We must share body heat tonight. If we build a fire, the man who shot you would find us. It will be cold tonight, and we do not have many blankets."

I lay between the two women, enjoying their warmth and the closeness of their bodies. This was different than the way I was raised. White women would freeze before they would share body heat from a man who was not their husband. Spring Flower and Night Dove took care not to reinjure my wounds. During the night when I could sleep on my back no longer, I tried to turn over on my side. They woke and helped me to find a new position; any little move I made would wake them.

When I woke the next morning, Two Mountains had the fire going and two rabbits cooking over the fire.

"Who shot you? Do you have enemies who wish you dead?" he asked.

After I told the story of my partners, my worry over my horse, and my escape, Two Mountains said, "No one has come through the pass. Your enemies must have given up. If they did not know you were injured, they would know that they would never catch your horse.

"We were hunting for food for the people in our camp, when we

9

found you. My people are starving," he explained. "There are no young men left to feed my people." He and the two young women had been gone three days hunting. They had not been able to find anything bigger than a rabbit.

"Where are the young men of your village? Have they gone out hunting and just not yet returned?"

"The Utes, who are our enemies, were on a raiding party. They came to our village and stole a bunch of our horses. Our young warriors prepared for war. The old wise men of our village tried to stop them from rushing to battle. The old ones knew that the Utes had left some of our horses that they could have taken. This is an old trick that the Utes used to lure the young warriors into a trap. They would leave a few horses so the braves would try to get the stolen horses back. The young warriors were eager to gain status among the tribe and would not listen. They wanted to dance around the fire, telling of their bravery. They called our old men 'women that stay in tepees.' The young braves told the old warriors to stay by the fire. 'We will protect you,' they said. Our young men did not see the trap until it closed in on them, killing them all. Now our people are starving. We need horses so we can hunt buffalo. If you will loan me two of your horses, I will go and bring back buffalo meat for my people."

When Two Mountains walked into the brush a little later, I called Spring Flower over and spoke of what the old warrior had told me. I felt like I needed to return the favor and help them. Without their help, I would probably have frozen last night or died from my wound, which felt much better this morning.

"Can he be trusted? Or will he trade my horses for whiskey?"

"Two Mountains is a good buffalo hunter, and our tribe needs buffalo meat. He would return. He has lost status in our tribe and is trying to gain it back. If you will let him use your horses, I will take you to our camp. Night Dove will go with Two Mountains to help him with the meat. They will return with your horses."

I knew that I had been between a rock and a hard spot when they had found me. They could have passed me by and taken my pack horses but chose to stop and help. I needed to trust and find new friends, for I had never planned to be here alone. And the girls seemed much more trustworthy than the trappers I had come west with. So I agreed with their plan.

"Two Mountains will hide your packs. He will hunt for buffalo. If that fails he will try to locate a friendly tribe we can join. He will bring your packs to camp when he returns," Spring Flower explained.

The next morning, she felt that we had to move. She helped me to get on Ollie.

"You need to move to the back of your horse and ride behind me."

I started to argue, but she already had a leg over Ollie before I knew what had happened.

"I know the way to our camp, and you need to hold on to me, instead of me trying to hold you up."

I knew this made sense, so I didn't argue with her.

Ollie did not like leaving the pack horses. They had followed him from St. Louis. It seemed not to matter that this young Indian woman was on his back. She had taken charge and headed them west. She held Ollie to a gentle pace for me, even though I knew she was in a hurry to return.

I put my arms around her to hold on. This was the only woman besides my mother who I had ever had my arms around. As she steadily guided Ollie through the trees and rocks, I begin to realize that this woman was a shade above what I had expected of Indian women.

Mathew had more or less talked of them as someone who did the work around camp and obeyed their husbands. He'd said that all you had to do was to give them a few trinkets and they would climb in the bed with you. I felt like he had not met these women.

This woman had come into my camp and taken charge and probably saved my life. Now she was riding my horse—a horse that no one but me had ever straddled. I doubted that a few trinkets would have an effect on her.

CHAPTER THREE

When the sun was a couple hours past midday, Ollie come to a stop. His ears were pricked forward to some bushes about two hundred yards up the hill.

"There in the bushes is an elk," she exclaimed.

"Let me off and hand me the rifle."

"You are not yet close enough to kill the elk. We must get closer."

I knew that I was not able to get closer, but that shot was well within my range. I had made shots at smaller game from farther than that before.

"I am not going to try to get any closer," I said, just before the big rifle fired. The elk jerked and acted like it would run. I thought at first I had missed, but it was an easy shot. Before I finished reloading, the elk took a couple steps and went down.

Spring Flower jumped from the horse. She was very excited. She had thought that I would miss and scare it away, but I had made a great shot.

"This will save my people. We must get this meat to them."

She helped me back on the horse and then ran the rest of the way to the dead animal. With her knife, she had started gutting it before I got to the elk. It was a large bull, and it would fill many bellies.

With the meat cut and ready to pack, Spring Flower took my hatchet and cut down two small saplings and made a travois. She then laid the hide on the travois and loaded the meat, wrapping the hide over it.

She had left a small portion of elk meat out. She made a fire and began to cook this meat for us to have for our meal.

I begin to think that Mathew had never been around Indian women.

This woman had moved from one project to another without complaining. She was always checking my wounds and making me comfortable.

I had watched her do all this knowing that she was weak from hunger. Knowing how hungry she was, I thought of the people back in their camp. They had not eaten in a while. She was working as hard as she could to get them food. I would ride behind her anywhere.

Tomorrow she would be taking me to their village. I had managed to help them, as she had helped me. I had no fear. I trusted she would not lead me into danger.

These were the first Indians I had met. But I felt the people who had talked on the bad side of these Indians must not have taken the time to learn how they had to live.

After we had eaten, she began to make a shelter under two spruce trees. She gathered up boughs that she had broken from the trees. She was spending a lot of time making the bed.

"You are doing a lot of work for something that we will leave in the morning."

"It will snow tonight. I will make our shelter good and dry. You do not need to get cold or wet. If you do, your fever may come back."

She worked on our shelter until dusk had settled around us.

"It may snow so much that we have to stay longer. Sometimes the early snows can be very bad."

This woman never stopped thinking. She had fixed our camp to last for several days. She had been taught since birth to survive.

"Tonight it will get very cold. Do not be afraid to hold me so our bodies will hold heat and be warm," she told me.

After she settled me in for the night, she lay down. With all the work that she had done that evening, I knew that she was very tired. I pulled her close, trying to keep her as warm as possible. She held me and was soon asleep. And soon after dark, the snowflakes begin to fall.

The next morning, no snow had made it to our blankets thanks to her hard work. I would bet that the trappers had not prepared the way that she had. Their blankets were probably wet from the snow, and their sorry butts were probably freezing. That bullet through my side may have saved my life. If I had not been shot, I would never have found my new friends and would probably be scalped by now.

13

After we had eaten our breakfast, we hooked the travois to Ollie. I got on and was moving back so she could get on.

"I will walk and clear the snow in front of Ollie." There again she was already doing things that I would not have thought about. If I was going to survive in these mountains, I was going to have to watch and learn as much as I could from these people.

Things were happening so fast. What were the herbs she had used on my wound? Things like that I needed to know. Maybe she would point them out for me before I left.

As we moved through the snow, Ollie walked in her tracks pulling the travois. It was about midday when we went across the mountain saddle back. We went another mile and then turned north. After an hour in that direction she turned east through spruce trees surrounded with cliffs in the shape of a horseshoe. As we came into a clearing, you could see nine tepees.

When the women and children saw that it was Spring Flower, they began to come closer. The old men stayed by the fire. They looked as if they were too weak to come greet us. We moved closer to the fire with the travois, bringing the meat for the people to see.

Ollie did not like all those people getting close to him, but I think that he was too tired to put up a fuss. We pulled all the gear from him and let him go to the spring and drink. While he was drinking, the children were busy clearing snow from the grass so Ollie could eat. The old men, as hungry as they seemed to be, only had eyes for the horse.

The women and old men were talking to me all at one time. They would eat well tonight thanks to this stranger. I did not know how to tell them that Spring Flower had made this possible by saving me and leading me here.

I was taken to a tepee by two women between the ages of twenty and thirty years old. They started to strip my clothes from me. I was trying to keep them on, but they were not to be overruled. When they had everything off me, one of the older women took them out. That was the last I saw of those clothes.

The younger girl began to give me a bath. She had a soft doeskin and dipped it in warm water and started to wash me. I reached for her hand to take the rag and wash myself. She slapped the back of my hand very hard and said something. I did not understand what she said, but I knew what

14

she meant. While she was washing me, the older girl came back in and watched while I was bathed. It was the first time I could remember being naked in front of anyone, and I was uncomfortable.

She then started to work on my wound. She was massaging it with her fingers and some kind of oil. She massaged hard enough to get the soreness and swelling out but not enough to start it bleeding. She pulled the cover back and motioned me to lie down. When I was lying down she rubbed her hand over my chest. She said a few words that I did not understand. She gave a shy smile, and as she was leaving, I thought she expected me to ask her to stay.

Outside, there was loud talking. I could hear Spring Flower speak above the other voices. That put a stop to the noise.

Later, Spring Flower brought me a bowl of food. It was boiled meat with wild onions and some kind of roots that I had never tasted. It was the best food I had eaten since I'd left St. Louis. When we had finished eating, she put the bowls outside and returned.

She brought more water and sat it down on the other side of the fire. She then stood and dropped her clothing. She stood there and washed, making a show of her beautiful body as if it was something she did everyday. She finished with her bath, took the water, and threw it outside. She returned, got in the bed with me, and lay back to rest her weary body. I would not bother her, for as excited as I was, I did not understand these people and did not want to start any trouble. She had indicated that she was with Two Mountains, but she was lying in bed with me with no clothing. To get my mind on other things, I asked her what the noise outside the tent earlier had been about.

"Some of the girls were arguing over whose lodge you would stay in. Since you are in the lodge that belongs to Running Doe, the older girl who tended your wound, she felt she should be sharing the lodge with you."

"Is she coming to stay with us?"

"No. I sent her to sleep in my lodge tonight."

"Why?" I asked. I was beginning to get frustrated.

Spring Flower was beginning to get frustrated also. "The old ones will settle it tomorrow. Go to sleep. We have worked long, and tomorrow will come soon." She snuggled up to me and fell asleep.

That night, I did not sleep very well. Her warm body was up tight against mine, but she had given no indication for me to do anything other than sleep.

The next morning, as we lay in our tent, I asked her if it was okay that she slept in no clothing with me when she was in camp with all these people.

"Having no clothing means nothing. When someone gets hot in the summer or needs to share body warmth, clothes are of no use. Is it a problem with you? I ask because the girls told me they had to fight you to get your dirty clothes off," she said with a smile.

"Well, as I have never had a wife, I am not used to being around women without my clothes on. So yes, it is a problem for me. Do you intend for me to walk around outside with no clothes on? For mine have been taken from me."

She raised the flap and spoke to someone outside. Running Doe, the owner of the lodge, appeared with some buckskins and a big smile on her face. She came forward to help me with the clothes, but Spring Flower said something and the girl left and did not seem to be in a very good mood.

I walked outside, and the warm sunshine felt good. The snow was already beginning to melt. As I walked around, the old people came up to me, and I was sure they were thanking me for the meat.

Running Doe brought me another bowl of food. I tried to tell her that I could eat no more. But she only tried harder to feed me. I took a couple bites, and then she opened the flap for me to enter her lodge.

Spring Flower had seen this and came over and spoke roughly to her, and she quickly closed the flap behind her.

"Will I have to protect you from these women all day? Will I have to stand guard to keep them from fighting over you?" asked Spring Flower.

By now, I was beginning to understand that I was a mighty hot item that was in very short supply.

As I walked around, I became a little concerned for the safety of the tribe. Someone could hide in the trees and shoot at them, and the teepees would be no match for a bullet. There was no way to retreat for the cliffs behind.

I was working my way to a cliff in back when I noticed a teepee. I had not noticed this when we first spotted the camp. It looked as if the skins were about to rot off and had been placed away from the rest. I was looking at it when three young girls came up carrying wood.

They did not say anything or look my way. They had water boiling with some meat, wild onions, and roots like I had the night before. I decided that I would have to ask what these roots were before I left to go trapping.

When I got to the cliff, there was an overhang that could be walled up in front to put up a good defense, if need be. I had no way of knowing if the Ute's would come back for the old ones left in camp. Their young warriors may return just to make sport of the weakened old men.

When I got back to camp, I explained my idea to Spring Flower.

"If your people walled up the overhang on the cliff. They could hold off an attack from the Utes. With some water and food, you could hold out for a long time."

"I will talk to the elders, but do not expect too much from them. They are so weak that, unless Two Mountains brings more meat, the elders themselves will go hungry. Many of them will be left behind. The food we have will be given to the strongest of my people, so they can survive. The old ones know they will die soon anyway."

I was shocked that the elders would die and do so willingly. Unless enough meat was brought in to make sure that the stronger ones had a chance to survive, the old men and women would not have food.

"They are old. Their sons have been killed. Even with food, it will be hard on the elders to keep up the next time the tribe moves. They are weak and will be left to die." Spring Flower explained that was the way of her people. It was best to try to save the ones who still had a little strength. They had a better chance.

"What about the three girls who have the old, torn teepee that sets off from the rest? Why are they not within the camp?" Their teepee looked as if rain and cold air would blow through it.

"Their parents died last year when they got caught in a snowstorm. They have no brother or young man to help them. If they are unable to get skins to repair their teepee, they will probably freeze this winter. They have no one to take them in. If you become a burden to the tribe, then you become an outcast. Everyone is starving; no one has anything to give."

As I made my way back to the lodge, my mind was no longer on the women that seemed to be trying to get me in their teepees. Now I knew the women of this camp were looking for a man so that they would not wind up like the three girls I had seen. These people had a hard life.

When I am able to go trapping again, I found myself thinking I can bring back meat and skins from time to time. My wound was healing rapidly, thanks to the healing medicine of the Indians.

Spring Flower had been giving me lessons on the healing and cooking plants. I was grateful, for I knew I would need them when I left to continue my journey.

I needed to leave as soon as my gear was returned. It was getting late in the season. If I was going to get a cabin built before it snowed, I could not stay here long. I had to find where the beaver were best for trapping before I could build a cabin. There was no way of knowing how far I would have to travel. This land was unknown to me.

I was thinking on all these things when, as one, the village seemed to be moving. They all seemed to be going toward the grove of spruce trees. As I looked, I saw Two Mountains and Night Dove. They had returned.

They had made two travois that were loaded with meat, and they also had packs on their backs. They must have killed two buffalo. The horses were worn out from the load. The meat would be cut up and divided among everyone.

When I looked at Spring Flower, she was already answering the question I did not have to ask. Yes, there would be enough meat to move to a stronger tribe.

Two Mountains was through unloading the horses. I turned them loose to graze with Ollie. Ollie acted glad to have his company back; these two horses had trailed him from day one. But more important, I had my packhorses back, taking that worry off my mind.

Two Mountains spoke as he came over to me. "With so much meat, I had no way of bringing the packs. I will go in the morning and bring them to camp. With the loan of your horses, you have saved the lives of my people. And we will have a feast tomorrow to honor you."

Spring Flower tended my wound that night and left without returning. I wondered why no woman came to my lodge that night, why none had offered themselves to me. Maybe the old ones had decided I did not need a woman to keep me warm, as I was getting better.

Maybe I would ask Spring Flower if she knew, for she seemed to be in charge, always giving orders or getting the work done herself. If the women were being held from me and I needed to know why, she would tell me.

Later that day, Two Mountains returned with my packs and horses in fine shape. He unloaded the horses and released them again with Ollie.

As the sun was setting, we were finishing our meal and beginning to gather round the fire to celebrate the good hunt, with song, dance, and stories of hunts past.

Spring Flower came and set down beside me. The old warriors tried to dance to show the brave deeds that they had done in their younger days. But they were weak, and their joints were stiff.

Two Mountains spoke to the tribe, and Spring Flower interpreted for me. He said that, with our new brother's help, they would be able to move. They needed to leave when the sun rose, and maybe they could catch up with the big herd. They would probably meet another tribe that was following the same herd for their fall hunt. This was what the elders had decided.

When he finished, he placed the elk and buffalo hides in front of me. "The elders feel that you should have them. You will need a lodge and warm clothes for the winter."

I thought of the three girls and the condition that they were in as the rest went to their lodges. I knew that I could not use the hides knowing that they were freezing.

Before I went to my lodge I carried the hides and lay them in front of the girls' teepee. I returned to my bed, but sleep would not come easily.

I thought of them; they were so poor and had no one to help them. They had not made a show as the others had done. I could not understand how they were able to haul the wood. But if they had no help, they would do what had to be done. I thought of hanging to Ollie with a hole in my side. You do what you have to do in order to survive. You do not expect someone else to carry your load.

My mind kept going back to those poor girls. The oldest was about my age, and I thought the other two were maybe a year or two younger. I knew that they would die on the trail unless someone helped them. Maybe the skins would help them in some way. I had done all I knew to do, and now it was time for me to be on my way. I feel asleep thinking of all the things I had to do before the snow came.

When I woke and stepped out, Two Mountains had caught my horses and was loading the travois with the meat that they had prepared. I walked over and asked, "What are you doing with my horses?"

"We haul the meat with the horses."

"You have made a mistake. I am not going with you. I am going to trap beaver. I will need my horses to carry my packs."

Two Mountains looked as he did the day they had found me—like he had no way to accomplish what he had to do.

He looked at me and said, "I really thought that you would spend the winter with us."

Then he looked at the rising sun in what seemed like deep thought. When he looked back at me he said, "If I take you to a valley that is full of beaver, a valley that no man has trapped, will you let me use your pack horses until I can return in the spring?"

Spring Flower had spoken of some of the things that Two Mountains had done, and now he was trying to make things right with the tribe.

I was beat. I could not say no to these people. They had saved my life. I saw the misery they were in, so I said, "You will have to help me haul my packs there. Then you can use them."

We hurried to unhook the travois. We needed to be under way. Two Mountains would take me to the valley, come back, and try to get his people to safety.

As we mounted and started to leave, I could see Spring Flower looking from behind the flap of her lodge. I thought that her eyes looked sad.

I would probably never see this woman again. She had saved my life. I felt that I owed her. I realized that I was going to be alone again, but from what I understood she shared her tepee with the old warrior. It would have been good to share her company and learn the things that I did not know. I now could only think of the cold nights that I would have shared in her warm bed.

I think we must have followed the trail for an hour when Two Mountains changed directions and started traveling down a canyon. After about one mile, he turned west and pointed to the cliff wall.

"There is the opening there. I will show it to you, but I will not go inside. The old ones said that, in the past, some Spanish men went in, and every warrior who went in to kill them never returned. No warrior that ever went inside came out. We do not enter. Take your packs in and see and then return the horses if what I have said is true."

When I came through the pass, I knew I needed to go no farther. It was the most beautiful valley I had ever seen. I could see a stream in the middle, going down the valley. There were large beaver ponds, and the land was cleared around the ponds. The beaver had cut the trees and left stumps sticking up for hundreds of years. I could understand why anyone would not come out. No one would want to leave this place. I unloaded the horses and returned them to Two Mountains.

Two Mountains thanked me and promised to return in the spring.

"When I return, would it be possible to bring some mares to breed with Ollie? I would bring some fine ones to go with your fine stallion. Our tribe is in need of the strong traits that Ollie has."

"I will see what you bring and then decide if any of your mares will be worthy of Ollie."

We said our good-byes, and he told me he would see me in the spring.

He talked as if he was going to return, but I was afraid I would never see my horses or his brood mares again. Still, it seemed like a small price to pay for my life. I was sure I could trap as many beaver as I could handle here. If I could get the pelts to rendezvous, I could buy more horses.

CHAPTER FOUR

I decided to leave the packs for now and find a place to build a cabin. I knew that I would need to get it built before the snow came again.

As I rode through the valley, I saw a lot of deer and elk tracks. I came to a small trickle of water coming down through some spruce and fir trees. It had to have been flowing for thousands of years. You could tell that it must always run because of the way that it had worn through the rocks. Following the stream, I was led to a small crack in the wall. The small stream of water trickled from the crack.

I found a spot of land that was flat and close enough to the water to build a cabin. There would be plenty trees there to work with. I could build the cabin with a good lean-to for Ollie. If I did not protect him from the elements, I would be in the same shape as the tribe.

I returned for my gear and loaded Ollie with the pack to set up camp. After I made the long walk back to the site, I decided that I would need to set up camp now and return the next day for the other pack. The long walk over the rough terrain had taken its toll.

As I lay out my bedding, I realized that my location had been a lucky find. With the cliff behind me, I had only to watch the front. With the stream close, I could dig out a small pool to take a bath. I could build a small shelter over it to keep it from freezing in the winter. I would turn this into a fine home. All it would take was a little hard work and time.

After I had eaten, I lay in my bed looking up at the stars. I was a long way from home, and I was alone. I thought of the fine life I had shared with my mother and father, but they were dead and buried. I was truly on my own for the first time in my life. What would become of me? I knew that I would have to adapt to this way of life and fast.

I had never lived in a place that had a winter like the one I had heard would surely come. I had to build a good cabin and build it quickly. I would need firewood and meat put up before it got too cold.

The sun was just clearing the eastern wall when I headed out to bring back my last pack. When I returned, I would start cutting trees for the cabin. I was anxious to start cutting and notching the logs. That would take the longest time. I was still weak and would have to be careful to not reinjure my wound, but I had no time to waste.

Nearing the location of my packs, I could see that they had attracted attention, and someone was setting beside them. I checked my rifle and pistol to make sure they were loaded and moved slowly forward. Two Mountains had said no one would enter, but someone had.

When I had gotten close enough, I could make out three girls—three skinny girls with what belongings they had been able to drag on a travois. Apparently they had chosen to follow me, hoping that, after I had given them the skins, I might help them. Or worse, the tribe had refused to let them follow.

I looked at them, knowing that I would not refuse to help them. But three girls had not been a part of my plans.

I remembered the stew that I had seen in their pots. Then I thought that, if I could keep them alive, they could help around the camp and cook more of that stew. Besides, I was beginning to believe in fate.

My mother had always been a strong believer in fate. Had I not benefited by raising Ollie, when everyone had said that I could not? By deciding to leave my partners, knowing that I would be alone? Fate seemed to be playing a big role in my life.

I loaded the packs on Ollie and hooked their travois behind him. When finished, I asked, "Do you speak any English?"

The oldest one made signs with her hands that I did not understand.

I signaled with my hand the sign that everyone understood—follow me. Our little party headed down the trail to my camp, the three walking behind. I thought that they must have followed yesterday and, when they found my packs, decided to wait until I returned. As we walked, the girls were constantly looking around, and I wondered if they were afraid of this valley like Two Mountains had been.

They were probably hungry. I had not brought anything to eat, as I was going to get my pack back to camp and start cutting trees.

When we got to camp, the girls looked around and seemed to understand that this was where I intended to make my camp. They begin to unload their travois. There were the skins that I had given them.

I had been put in a position that I had not asked for, but my upbringing would not allow me to mistreat these young women. I got before them and put my hand on my chest and said. "Zack." I did not have to say it but a couple of times before they were pointing and saying my name.

The oldest put her hand on her breast and said a name that I knew I would not be able to pronounce or remember. I stopped her and pointed to her and said, "Annie." I had to repeat it a couple times before she understood. But when she did, she then pointed to the second girl and waited until I named her Beth, and the youngest I called Susie. These were names from my past, and I would not forget them soon.

CHAPTER FIVE

I had started to unpack some of the tools that I would be needing. When I brought out the Dutch oven, the girls began to chatter and picked it up and looked at it very carefully. I had an idea that they knew what it was for.

I realized that all I had for them to eat was some dried elk meat. I gave them some but knew that my plans had been changed. Now I must go out and get more meat.

I must start thinking ahead like Spring Flower would have done. Starting out with the skins they had, I could get a few more. And if we had to, we could build an Indian lodge.

I picked up my rifle and went back down the trail to try and locate something to keep us in food for a while.

I was thinking that I had been dealt a new hand—different than the one I'd had when I'd left St. Louis. Maybe if these girls were able to work, they could help with the cabin. But right now I had to feed them and get some meat on their bones.

I suddenly saw a buck about one hundred yards away that I had almost missed. I'd had the girls on my mind, trying to figure out the things that I would need to do and had not been paying attention. I raised my rifle and waited for a sure shot. The powder and lead was too important to waste. I had no idea when I would be able to get more. I raised my rifle and dropped the buck. I had barely got to the place it had dropped before the girls showed up. They pushed me aside and began to butcher the deer, and it was a good thing. Most of it, I would have thrown away. But they wasted nothing.

As I watched them work, knowing how weak they were, I could not help but be amazed. Annie spoke to the other two. They loaded the meat on their backs and headed for camp. No squabble; just get it done.

I knew that I needed to learn their language, and they needed to learn mine. I felt that it would be good to have someone to talk with if they chose to stay. Then during the long winter months, we could work on learning each other's language.

When we returned to camp, they immediately began cooking and preparing the meat to be stored.

Seeing that I was of no use, I got my ax and bucksaw and walked into the timber. I had my first tree down and begin to cut the limbs. As weak as I was, I could not work very hard. But I could not stop; winter was on its way.

Out of nowhere, Beth, the second girl, came and began to drag limbs out of my way. I saved a lot of energy moving around without having to climb over them, and she was piling them for future use as firewood.

I decided that now was a good time to start teaching her a few words. I walked over to a tree and called Beth. When she looked toward me, I motioned for her to join me. I put my hand on the tree and said, "Tree," until I was sure she understood.

"Tree," she would reply.

Then I went to the log that I had cut off and said, "Log."

Beth shook her head no and said, "Tree."

I went back and pointed to the tree, naming it, and then back to the log, naming it to show her there was a difference.

After watching me go back and forth, Beth pointed to the tree saying, "Tree." Then she would point to a log and say, "Log."

As I cut and trimmed the trees and logs, she would say the names, showing me she understood and was prepared to learn more.

Annie, having food ready, sent Susie to bring us to camp to eat. When we came into camp, I saw it had been organized.

The Dutch oven was full of the stew that I had eaten in their Indian camp. They had made a backrest and leaned it against a tree. They motioned for me sit down and lean back. Annie dished up a bowl of stew for me. It was as good as it smelled, and I ate my fill. Susie kept trying to get me to eat more.

I knew not to overstuff myself with food with all the work I had to do.

As I left to go back to work, Annie spoke to Beth and Susie, who got up and followed me, while she made herself busy cleaning up.

After I got back, I took the ax and begin to cut the notches in the log. I cut a small sapling to the correct length for my notches.

When I had notched them all, I began to cut more down. Then I would notch them. Beth saw what I was doing, and when I cut another tree down, she grabbed the ax and began notching the log. I watched to make sure that she did not cut it wrong. It had taken a lot of work to put the tree on the ground. She did as good a job as I could have done; she even went around to the logs already notched, I guess to see if she had done it correct. I looked at her and gave a smile of gratitude. She returned it with one that I thought said we were going to get along fine.

When Annie came and joined us, Beth took her and Susie and explained the words she had learned.

Earlier that morning, I had swung the ax wrong and almost cut my foot. I had not really paid any attention to what I had said until Beth picked it up and later said to the other girls, "Damn ax." I almost fell over laughing and chose not to correct them because they were learning on their own.

At the end of the day, we were so much farther along than I expected. I could see us getting it finished before a big snow hit.

That evening, when we returned to our camp, they started the cooking fire and getting things around camp done.

After we had eaten, I called them over. With my hands, I motioned for them to sit, and then I started to teach them new words. They understood that it was important and began to work together to pick it up faster. Beth may remember a word that the other two had forgotten, and the others might pick up on some words she missed.

As the days went along, the girls had learned a lot of words, like *bring*. I would say maybe, "Bring my knife."

Beth had returned from getting water and told Annie to bring the damn ax. I could not help but laugh when I heard it, and hearing me laugh, they begin to laugh also.

I think that was when we began to really bond. Maybe before they were trying only to pay their way. Maybe they were a little frightened of me. Now things had changed. They seemed to understand that we would get through this together.

CHAPTER SIX

When I felt we had enough logs cut and dragged to the site, we began to put them in place. With the girl's help, the cabin went up fast. I had taught them how to mix clay with straw and water and then pack it into the cracks to keep the cold air from blowing through.

For several evenings after we ate, we would walk down to the beaver ponds and look around. Along the way, I would teach a new word and answer the best I could their questions—when they could make me understand what they were asking.

The cabin was up. I was building the fireplace. If I got up and walked away to stretch my legs or just to do something different, they would take my place and keep the work moving. We had the roof on and the fireplace finished. The girls explained to me that, in their camps, it was the women's job to build the homes. It did not seem right to them that I felt I had to help.

Now I was trying to make a table and a bench to set on. Later, I would start on beds and maybe some stools.

The girls were busy bringing the wood to the shed, like squirrels gathering acorns. They did not let any time go by that they were not preparing for the cold winter that was threatening.

We had put up plenty of food for the winter, and the girls had begun to mend. We did not have to work so hard now that we had our cabin and sheds built. They were regaining the weight that they had lost while living on their own.

We were able to hold a better conversation with each other now. We would sit by our fireplace and watch the fire burn. Where I had constantly worried about having everything ready for winter, now we were able to slow down, and I begin to think of the future.

One evening, we were sitting in front of the fire. Annie had gotten up to bring me water. When she returned and sat down, the light reflected off her in a way that I could see her beauty. Until that moment, I had not noticed. I guess I had in my mind that they were still those starving young women they'd been when I'd first met them. They were not beautiful like Spring Flower had been, but as they gained their weight back, you could tell that they would be.

Annie caught me looking at her. I guess that it was the first time I had looked at her that way. She just acted as though she had not noticed.

Annie was quieter than the other two girls. She had learned responsibility early.

She had been taking care of the three of them by herself, when they had no one to help them. She seemed to be more thoughtful of others, always making sure that everyone had plenty of warm clothes or food before she would do for herself.

When the snow began to fall and the cold winter wind began to blow, at night we would pile up in one bed as Spring Flower had done with me.

We would laugh, usually at something Susie would say or do. She always seemed to know when to do or say something funny. It was usually Beth that might get angry, if she felt she was the one who had done a thing that the rest of us thought was funny.

CHAPTER SEVEN

Beth had made friends with Ollie, and she seemed to have the same connection with him that I had. If Beth thought Ollie had not been tended to just right, she would get angry. From day one, she had stayed with Ollie as much as possible.

One day I came out, and she was rubbing him down. She had put some kind of oil or grease on him. As she rubbed it with a piece of doeskin, it made his coat shine. She said it was so, when it rained, the water and ice would shed from his fur.

She asked, "Do you know what a great horse he is? He should have many colts."

I told her, "Ollie and I have not spent enough time in one place to think about having colts, but Two Mountains is suppose to bring mares in the spring. I am looking for only the best and strongest mares to breed to him."

She seemed to be happy with what my plans were.

I began to set what few traps I had managed to get away with when I had left the trappers. At first I was having no luck. Each day, I checked the traps to find them empty.

Beth followed me one day and showed me what I was doing wrong. When I began to bring beaver and other pelts home, the girls would scrape and tan them. We caught a lot of rabbit and mink. Annie was busy making coats for us.

One day when Beth and Susie were out checking beaver traps with me, I asked, "Will the two of you make Annie a warm coat from some of the fur? She has made each of us a fine coat but nothing for herself."

I did not know if she thought she was being too free with the skins that we were bringing into our cabin. I did not want her to feel I did not trust her to do what was best for all of us. I asked them why she had not taken more for herself when I was bringing in enough for everyone.

They looked at each other with their little knowing smiles and set about making a beautiful coat. When they finished with it, Beth said, "Here is the coat for Annie. The best time to give it to her is when you are alone. It will mean so much more to her coming from you."

We had finished our meal. Beth asked Susie to come outside and help with Ollie. I wanted to surprise Annie with the coat. I had her turn away and close her eyes, and I think it actually frightened her. I lay the coat over her shoulders. At first she looked as if she were in shock. Then she hugged me for the first time. She thanked me with a smile on her face that said everything. I thought I saw a tear roll down her cheek.

When it was time to go to bed, she spoke to Beth and Susie, and they took their bedding to the loft. I got in bed, wondering if they had decided to start sleeping in the loft. I would miss sharing the warmth of their bodies in our bed.

As the fire burned down and Annie finished with her work, she sat down before the fire and shook the braids from her hair. I did not know it was so long and beautiful. The girls had kept their hair in braids.

She came to my bed and dropped her clothing and got in bed with me. She came close and held me in her arms and said, "Tonight I become your wife."

She helped me get my clothes off, and I began to realize that it was not for warmth. I had no idea of what she expected of me, but nature took over, and I did the best I could. Afterwards, I was ready to go to sleep. I soon found out that I was in for a very long night—one I knew I would never forget.

When we woke, the next morning, Beth and Susie had gone outside, probably to hunt for rabbits. Annie and I got untangled, and she got up, putting on her clothes. I saw what a beautiful woman she had become before my eyes. The night before she had combed out her hair and let it down. Now she was combing it out, and it hung well down her back. While I lay in bed watching her, she began to braid it back. I asked her, "Can you leave your hair down?"

She stood up, walked back to bed, and dropped her clothing, turning around as if to show me what a woman she had become.

"Whatever you want. You are my husband, and I want to make you happy." There is no way to explain how beautiful she was. I pulled the cover back and she came to me, and we made love again.

"Are you happy with me, my husband?"

I thought of the skinny girls that I was so sure would have died on the trail traveling to another camp. I thought of the suffering that they had gone through.

"I want you to stay with me come spring. I will take care of you and your sisters," I told her.

CHAPTER EIGHT

The following days and weeks were happy times. The girls continued to bloom and blossom into beautiful young women. We had put up plenty of food to get us by, and I was still bringing in fresh beaver. The girls had made bows and arrows and began to kill small game.

They seemed to be happy that I had made their sister my wife. Annie seemed to enjoy her role more than ever. We continually worked on the cabin, making it warmer and building things that made life easier.

When spring returned, I started making a corral to hold Ollie. If I was able to get some mares I wanted to have the mares breed at different times. I needed to know when they were bred so I would know when and what order they would fowl. I would be able to hold them in the corral and help if they had trouble.

Beth had always liked to be around the work that I was doing. She did not care to be cooking or doing housework. When we put Ollie in the corral, I said, "We will have to fix a way for him to always have water." She picked up the pickax from the tool shed and started cutting a trench from our stream to his corral. It took some hard work, and I knew that she would not stop until she had it like she wanted. I grabbed my shovel and went to work. When we had finished, we had brought the stream to a rock that had an indention in the top. The hole would hold about five gallons of water and would stay full. This would allow the horses to drink from it, and it would continue to refill.

We had finished the work that I had planned, with a little time to spare. I had been wanting to explore the valley. It seemed so big and beautiful, but with all the work we had been doing, I just had not gotten around to exploring.

As I looked down the valley, I had an idea. I called to Annie, asking her, "Would you like to join me? We will spend a few days exploring the valley."

She asked, "Did you ask Beth to go? This is something she would love to do."

I told her, "I want you to join me as my wife. We will camp and enjoy each other's company. You are always working in the house. This will be time for just you and me."

I felt like Annie, for some reason, did not want to make the trip. I wanted her with me, and she must have seen it in my eyes, for she said, "I would love to go."

When I came inside, Annie was packing the things that we would need. I noticed a different attitude from Beth. I knew that Beth would have loved to go because that was just the thing that Beth loved to do.

When we were on Ollie and going out of site, Annie said, "Beth really wanted to go. I hope that she will be all right."

I answered, "I know Beth was upset, but I really wanted you with me on this trip. I love Beth. But when we are working and doing things, she takes charge. She does not seem interested in what I want to do. She will change what I told her to do to what she wants done. I really wanted you to come along and hear my ideas and for us to be alone for a few days."

Annie smiled, knowing this was true. Beth always wanted things her way.

We had traveled for about an hour when the land became flat. The area was about five miles wide and about ten miles long; occasionally there would be a grove of trees. There was enough grass that a man could have a large herd of cattle.

With people already coming—and surely more would come—they would need good horses to ride and beef to eat. If they could see the beautiful landscape that I was looking at, they would come in swarms.

As I explained it to Annie, she said, "I would rather it stay like it is now. We have everything we need. When you get more colts and raise them, we can ride over this valley and spend time like now. I know of nothing else that we would want."

We decided to ride up against the nearest canyon wall to look for a place to camp. It was getting late, and dusk would soon be settling in. We came upon a branch of water when she spotted an object sticking out of the ground.

I helped her from the horse, and we moved the dirt to uncover it. It was a piece of what I thought was copper or brass shaped like a turtle shell. I tried to remember where I had seen something like it before. I had the feeling that I knew what it was but could not really be sure.

We decided to make camp there and look for more objects that would explain what we had found. While she was making camp, I went back to the spot where we'd found the piece. With the first scoop, I hit something else under the dirt. As I removed the soil from it, I knew what it was—a Spanish helmet. Two Mountains had spoken of Spanish men who had entered this valley but not returned.

I showed it to Annie saying, "This one must have died, and the others buried him before they left."

Annie said, "No, none of them came out. There was no other way in or out according to the old ones."

The Spanish had captured many of the Indians and had forced them to work for them. When the warriors found where they had been taken, the warriors had gone into the valley to rescue their family members. But no one ever returned.

"Maybe the warriors that followed attacked, and everyone was killed," I suggested.

"No one knows," she replied, "because when our warriors did not return, our wise man said it was bad medicine. After that, all of our warriors were afraid to go inside."

Annie had gotten out the jerked meat and was leaning back on a rock. When I saw how beautiful she was, I remembered why I had wanted her to come. I took her hand and led her to our bed and helped drop her clothing.

After a few days in the valley, we decided to work our way back to our cabin. We packed the armor we had found and brought it to show Beth and Susie.

CHAPTER NINE

We had enjoyed our trip but were glad to get home.

Beth took the armor and put it on Susie so we might tell what it would have looked like.

Beth took it outside and attached it to the corral fence and shot it with her bow. The arrow glanced off into the timber. When she retrieved the arrow, the head had been shattered. I decided that it was much harder than copper—that it was probably brass. Beth took it and cleaned it up. After she had it clean enough, she made straps to fasten it over her body.

Beth and Susie took turns trying the armor on. They would use a stick to hit each other where the armored covered them to see if they would feel any pain.

One night we were sitting by the fire and talking about how the land looked where we had found the rest of the armor. I said, "I have been thinking; if we had a cabin in that valley, when we get our horses, we could keep them in the deep grass and stay in the cabin while we trained our horses."

"We should start it soon," said Beth. You could see how excited she was about the idea.

Annie was hesitant. "This cabin is where we have first known happiness. I do not want to leave it."

"We will not leave it forever. We will have to have a place to stay when we return." I assured her that we would keep the cabin.

I had not said anything about building a stronghold at the new cabin site. But it was on my mind—just in case the Utes found our valley. I did not want to alarm the women, but I was beginning to worry more about my growing family. I could no longer just pick up and leave. I had lives around me that I had come to love, and I had to protect them.

During the night, I woke at the sound of Ollie snorting. It was as if he was warning whatever was there to stay away. My first thoughts were of the Utes.

I grabbed my pistol and rifle. I eased the door open so no light would escape and give away my position. I stepped outside, not leaving the door completely until I had a handle on what was out there and giving my eyes time to adjust to the darkness.

I thought that Ollie would either jump the fence or tear it down. I had never seen him so agitated. Something was out there that had him upset. With him quieted, I could hear more horses. I was afraid that our location had been found.

My first thought was to get in the shelter where I could defend my family if we were attacked. I realized that Ollie had given away our position. I opened the gate and let him out. He would stand a better chance if he was not confined. If there were Indians out there, they would want to catch this beautiful horse. But out in the open, they would not be able to get close to him.

Ollie went straight for the spot I had heard the other horses. I thought that he would run, and they would give chase. But when he got there, all hell broke loose. I was almost crying, fearing that I had let him go into danger, rather than him leading it away from us.

I started to follow when a hand stopped me. I had not realized that Beth had joined me. When I realized that it was her, I noticed that she had put on the Spanish armor.

I almost laughed at first, but I saw the serious side of her. She had her bow and arrows and had come to my aid.

I grabbed her. "Go back into the cabin. I do not know who is here. I have heard horses, but have seen no one."

"If there is a fight, it will be outside, not in a cabin. And I will be a part of it," replied Beth.

The noise quieted down with just the sound of horses running. They were headed for the entry of the canyon.

Beth, listening, said, "These are wild horses. They have either killed Ollie, or he has joined them."

"How do you know it is just horses?"

"No war party stirs this time of night. If it were friendly warriors, they would have waited until we were up and outside. If it was a war party, they would have struck at the first light. Probably it was wild horses, and Ollie has left with them."

We remained outside the rest of the night, and just before the break of day, Beth leaned against a fence post and went to sleep.

With the sun coming up, I saw Beth in her armor, her bow in hand. She had come out to fight and help protect our family and property. I realized in that moment how much of my life she had become.

Whatever I was doing, whether it was hunting meat, fixing fence, or preparing for war, she was by my side. At that moment, I wanted to take her in my arms and hold her as close as possible.

When full daylight came, we made our way to the place we had heard the horses last night.

There were many unshod horse tracks and two sets of shod horses. One was surely Ollie—it was the biggest one—but one was smaller. It was either a mare or a much smaller male.

Beth said, "I think we have lost Ollie. Do you think we will ever see him again?"

I lay my arm across her shoulder and told her that, if there were any way, he would come back. Walking back toward the cabin, she did not try to separate from me, but instead, with her free hand, held my hand that lay across her shoulder.

When we reached the cabin, Annie and Susie stepped out. I removed my arm, and a hurt look came across Beth's face. Annie came to meet us and, with Beth walking between us, asked me to explain what I thought had happened.

I was kind of surprised that Annie did not even give me a strange look. Had it been my father walking up with his arm around another woman, there would have been hell to pay at our house. But I had done it unaware of what I was doing, and maybe Annie knew that.

CHAPTER TEN

Over the next three weeks, we had to change our plans about starting the new cabin. Without Ollie, we could cut the trees, but we would not be able to move them. I had my ax and bucksaw out sharping them so when Ollie returned—and I fully believed that he would if he was able—we could start the new cabin. I didn't know what I would do with no horse. Maybe Two Mountains would return soon.

I was just finishing up when I heard the thunder of horses coming toward the cabin. There were five horses ahead of Ollie, and he was driving them toward us.

When they got closer, four of them kind of shied away. But the one with the shoes on went right in the corral and begin to drink water. She was used to being in a confined place.

Slowly, with Ollie pushing them, the other horses moved to the corral and drank water. They milled around, and after seeing there was no way out, they began to settle down.

Beth had joined me. "Ollie has brought his family back. He must have run the other stallion away."

When he came closer, we were able to see that he had been in a fight. He was not hurt too badly—just a few bite marks.

Beth grabbed her oil and rubbed the marks on Ollie, scolding him like a little child. He acted as if he knew he deserved it.

She had a way with him. Until Spring Flower, Ollie would not let anyone around him without me by his side, keeping him calm.

I looked the horses over. Ollie had brought all mares. The strange thing was, there were no colts. None of the horses looked as if they were bred.

Back in Mississippi, we had a bull with our cows but never got a calf from him. We had to get a new one. Pa said the bull was sterile. It may have been that the stallion with the mares had not been able to get the mares bred.

When Beth finished with Ollie, she was able to get the mare with the shoes to come to her. She rubbed her down, and all the time, Ollie kept following her, wanting to be rubbed down more. Beth had spoiled him, and he wanted her attention.

Annie and Susie had heard the sound of horses running and had come out to see what was going on.

"Ollie has returned and brought us a herd of mares. In a few days, we will lead them to the deep grass in the valley. Then as nature takes its course, we will begin to have baby colts. Now we must start our cabin, so we can be near them."

"Will they not leave when we turn them out?" asked Annie.

"We cannot keep that many horses in our pens. We will be unable to feed them. They will have time to get used to us. Then we will lead them to the deep grass."

Beth said, "I will keep the mare that has shoes and Ollie together. I will hold them until I am sure the mare is bred. I will train the mare to be our riding horse."

Annie looked at me to see if that was true.

I shrugged my shoulders and said, "She is the one who knows horses."

"You have given her the perfect name," said Annie with a big smile on her face.

I thought of how easily it had come and knew it fit.

"Come here Beth," called Annie. "Zack has you a new name."

She looked puzzled, and I said, "If you like the name, we will call you, One Who Knows Horses."

Knows Horses wrapped her arms around my neck and kissed me as I had kissed Annie. When she released me, I stepped back, heat coming to my face. I felt what she had done was out of happiness, but I felt that Annie's patience might be wearing thin.

The next day, I took Ollie out to try to kill some fresh meat. Annie wanted some hides to scrape. After getting meat and hides for Annie, Knows Horses and I would begin to cut logs for the new cabin.

On my return, when I had gotten close enough to see the cabin. I saw what I thought was the wild mares tied to trees around the cabin. Knowing Knows Horses, I had no doubt that she had done it. But on second look, I saw these horses were different.

Spring Flower stepped out of the cabin and ran to meet me.

"I have returned with your pack horses and two mares that Two Mountains was able to trade for."

"I had not expected to ever see you or my pack horses again," I told her. "I was afraid that you would have run into trouble. Did your tribe find buffalo? Were you able to find a new tribe?"

"We almost made it with everyone. But some of the elders, knowing their time was near, lay down and refused to be a burden on the rest. After a week of following the buffalo herd, we met some of our kin and joined with them. We have wintered well and have gotten many beaver pelts."

Spring Flower said, "You made a good choice while in our camp, giving Annie your hides. Is she not a good wife?"

"What does that have to do with anything? The girls were freezing at your camp? I could not keep my hides and let them die. Then they came to me starving, and I could not refuse them. Has this caused trouble among your people?"

Spring Flower explained, "When you took the hides to Annie's tent, it was a gift. As the girls had no father, she accepted your gift on behalf of them. When Two Mountains returned with the pack horses, she told him that they would accept your offer. He told them where he had taken you."

"I had given the hides to three starving girls. It was not my intent to buy a wife. I did not know the way of your people. But I am very happy with Annie as my wife."

Spring Flower, laughing, said, "You did not buy just Annie to wife but the other two also. You will have three fine wives."

Annie and Susie were coming to join us. Annie said, "Spring Flower and Two Mountains are going to rendezvous. Do you want to take your furs and join them?"

I asked Spring Flower if she would be able to take my pelts and pick up our supplies. "I am going to be busy with the new cabin, and I do not want to leave the women alone," I explained.

"Yes I will take them to trade. I will return with your supplies. I will not let Two Mountains buy whiskey with them."

We had the two pack horses loaded when Spring Flower came to me. "I understand why you give Annie the gift," she told me. "I had hoped that you would bring the hides to my tepee that night."

"When I gave that gift, I had no way of knowing I was buying a wife. Besides, are you not Two Mountains's wife?"

"No. I only agreed to let him stay in my lodge to bring in meat. Two Mountains had encouraged me to go with you and get with child. He is too old to give me the child that I will need to help me when I get older. I have no husband and will become an outcast."

I had forgotten most of what I had learned while I was with these people. I had been teaching the girls my way of life, and I had not learned much about theirs.

Spring Flower seemed to be sadder since I had last seen her. I felt that she had been burdened with the others, as she was always taking care of everyone else.

"If you ever need help, come to us, and you will have a home."

As she was leaving, I was thinking about how she had saved my life. At the same time, she was looking after the whole tribe, trying to get them to safety.

I thought about what she had said about wanting me to leave the hides at her teepee. I felt bad about it, but I had not known their customs. I did not know Spring Flower did not belong to Two Mountains. Had I made a mistake?

If I had not left my hides at Annie's lodge, I would not have known the love that she and I shared. I did not think, even if I could, I would change the way that I had handled it. Saving these three women had, in fact, saved me. I don't think I would have lived through the winter here without them.

CHAPTER ELEVEN

Before the visit, I had been happy about starting the new cabin. Now I could not get my mind off the past. We had been so happy we had forgotten that the rest of the world was out there. I went in the house to find Annie, telling her what I had learned from Spring Flower and that I was glad she had followed me.

"I have invited Spring Flower to return if she needs help. I feel I owe her. She saved my life."

"I would be happy for her to return. She worked hard to keep everyone fed and warm in our village, but we were too weak at the time to give her much help."

I felt better after talking with her and made plans to go ahead and start the cabin as we had planned. I went to the corral to tell Knows Horses that we would be starting the cabin the next day.

She was rubbing the mare down when I came in. She asked, "Can I ride this mare? She is not used to being inside, she needs to run with the wind."

"The horse is yours," I told her. "You can do with her as you feel is best."

I don't think if I had given her Ollie she would have been any happier.

That night, I think Annie made love to me more than I to her. After, when we were lying in each other's arms, Annie said, "Tomorrow you will make Knows Horses your second wife."

I did not know what I should say or do.

Annie did not seem happy with the delay in our conversation. "Do you not love her? Has she done something to offend you? Knows Horses has waited patiently. You gave her a name and a horse. She will expect it."

"What are your feelings about me taking Knows Horses for a wife?"

"We have always known that we would share a husband. And we were happy when we realized it would be you." Annie pulled me close and said, "Tomorrow I want my sister to feel what I have felt with you in my arms. I want her to know that you have accepted her as your wife. She has worked with you but has not shared your bed. Let her know that she will always have a home."

The next morning, Ollie and Knows Horses were ready to leave for the valley. The packhorse was loaded. I was trying not to seem aware of the happiness the girls were sharing. I made a show of making sure that the packs were tied securely. I went to Annie and kissed her good-bye. Then I went to Susie, hugged her, and said good-bye.

As Knows Horses and I were leaving, I worried about leaving the others behind. We may be gone for a couple of weeks. If they had the new rifles that Spring Flower was to bring back from rendezvous, I would feel better. They had their bows, and I had piled green wood to burn if they needed us to return. I had placed green wood behind the cabin and in front of the cliff. If someone tried to harm them, maybe one could get to the wood and set it afire. The darker smoke would go up in front of the white cliff, making it easy to see from our camp.

As we traveled, at first, we made nervous small talk. Knows Horses was always ready to make changes when things were not going the way she wanted. She said, "Do you want me for your wife?" She had the ability to come to the point.

I was a little embarrassed but knew that it was time to talk. "In my culture, a man only takes one wife, and I have never expected more. I have thought that I loved you, and the morning that Ollie left was when I knew for sure. But I do not love Annie any less. I do know that I want you for a wife, but it may take a while before I can treat you like I treat Annie."

"Do Annie or Susie love horses?"

"No. They did not seem interested in them."

"Do I like the blue flowers that grow by the spring?"

"Only to feed the horses with."

"Then do not try to treat me in the same way. Treat me as the wife that you will come to know in time. This is why Annie wanted us to come alone. You will know me as your second wife. You will learn the things that we enjoy doing together. We can do them without thinking of anyone else."

"What will happen when we are back and it is time to go to bed?"

Knows Horses said, "We will handle that among ourselves. This is not new to us. Our village has always had sister wives, and it works well for us."

We rode in silence for a while before I asked, "Do you have any plans for our new cabin? As my wife and trainer of our horses, you will live here more than the rest."

And in typical Knows Horses style, she had already been thinking of new ways to make this cabin better than the one we now had. "We will have to make a room for children. And we'll have a cover for the front porch so we can sit in the shade in the hot summer. And in the winter we can sit in the early morning sun."

She was excited. The closer we got, the more she talked about what she wanted. She would be able to have a say in this cabin. This would be her home, and she wanted to design it for herself.

We had arrived at the site, and she still sat on the mare, pointing where she wanted the cabin and how she wanted it to face.

I was off Ollie, standing beside the mare listening to her talk. I suddenly realized that this beautiful woman was soon to be my wife. I reached for her and pulled her from the horse. I held her close and kissed her long. "I am glad that you know what you want. But in order to build this cabin, we will have to get to work and not just talk about it."

It was well past midday, and she wanted to go to the place where we had found the armor. We unloaded the packhorse and rode about two miles to the spot. When we arrived, she walked around, looking for more items that might be hidden under the loose dirt. We found things—some cooking pans and another chest plate. Knows Horses came over to me and said, "I will make you a beautiful necklace of this." She held out her hand and showed me an object.

I took it from her, examining it closely. "Where did you find this?"

"I went back to where the chest plate was found and dug in the dirt. Do you know what it is?"

"It is what white men called gold."

"What is gold?"

"It is something that will make us rich, if we could find more of it."

"What is rich?"

"We want to raise fine horses, trade them for guns and things that we need. But in the white man's world, we could take gold and buy what we wanted."

It was getting late, and we had work to do tomorrow. We went to our camp and finished fixing our food and getting the camp in order. I was going to build a lean-to like Spring Flower had made.

Knows Horses said, "Tonight, we will sleep under the stars." She dropped her clothing, walked to the stream, and started to take her bath. When she finished, she motioned me into the water. She began to bathe me. I pulled her close, and as cold as the water was, it felt like her body was on fire. She looked in my eyes and said, "I will wait no longer." I carried her to our blankets, and she proved that night that I would always treat her differently.

Early the next morning found us cutting trees. I felt bad thinking about Annie. I realized that I would have to remember that this was what the sisters and their people had done for hundreds of years to guarantee that they would survive. Perhaps the sisters wanted this way of life. I would keep an eye on how things changed when we were all together again.

Work went well, and when I would set down to rest, Knows Horses brought me water. We began to talk about the things we wanted to do with the horses.

"If we could find enough gold, we could buy all the things we will need," I told her.

"Did you not say that, if the white men heard we had gold, they would come and hunt for it and destroy everything we have here to find it?"

"This is true. Our valley would be overran with miners everywhere. They would probably build cabins to stay in and, eventually, a town of some kind. All kinds of men would follow—some good and some like the ones who shot me. Soon we would be forced to leave. This valley would no longer be ours."

"I do not know of the things that you want to buy. We have more than we ever had. All we need is here."

She stood and dropped her clothes and stood before me. She said, "I would not be able to do this with so many people around." She then laid me back and made love to me. As we lay cuddling, she told me, "Never speak of this gold again—not even to my sisters."

The work was progressing along. We were already dragging the logs to the cabin site, and we missed Annie and Susie. With my mind on them, I asked Knows Horses, "Do you know a new name that I might call Annie or Susie?"

"When you gave me a new name, where did it come from?" she asked.

"It was something that I just said, and it seemed to fit."

"When you find a name, you will know it. You cannot just think of something and make it fit. The name must come from your heart. When you give a name, the person you named will know that it is special and will honor it."

CHAPTER TWELVE

The day had come when it was time to start laying the logs in place, and we would need help. We had risen early and were going to bring Annie and Susie to join us. We were eager to get home. We had been gone ten days and were beginning to worry about the other half of our little family.

I realized that it was going to be hard to face Annie, but it had to be done. I had really enjoyed what Knows Horses and I had shared. We had worked and made love, and I understood that Knows Horses was a different person than Annie or Susie. And I would treat her as Knows Horses. I would also remember and treat the other two as their personalities required.

Annie and Susie came running to meet us. They hugged each other. Annie held me and kissed me in a way that told me that tonight would be special if I did not do anything to screw it up. She released me, and the three girls went in the house laughing and talking in their language. I felt that they did not want me to know what they were talking about, and I was fine with that, as long as Annie was happy.

We talked long into the night about the new cabin. Knows Horses explained all the improvements that she wanted to make, and the other two had a few ideas also.

Finally they started to bed. I was wondering how this was going to work when Knows Horses told Susie to come to bed with her.

I climbed in bed, watching Annie take her hair down and comb it out. When she stood before the embers that were left of the fire, she dropped her clothing. She reminded me that she was a beautiful woman. She came to bed, and it was like the first night I held her—never wanting to let go. How could I explain to her how much I loved her?

The next morning, Knows Horses and Susie came down before we got up. Knows Horses lay down beside me, and Susie lay next to Annie, giving each of us a big kiss, telling us how happy they were. We lay there for a while, just loving life.

We finally got up and started to prepare to leave for the new cabin. It did not take long to pack up. Since we were not leaving until the next day, we had most of the day left.

I had been wanting to climb the cliff for a while—to see if I could find the source of the stream that never stopped flowing.

When I told the girls of my plans, they were eager to join me. Soon we set out to find a way that we might be able to get to the top. We spent the biggest part of the day exploring, but we were never able to get very high. The day was great fun, but we accomplished little.

The next morning, as we were making sure that all our packs were tight, Spring Flower came, leading the packhorses and bringing the new rifles. We all were happy to see her and had forgotten that they would be returning.

"Where are you headed?" she asked.

"We are going to the new cabin that Zack and Knows Horses have been building. They have done all they can without our help," replied Annie.

"Can I join you? I would love to see the new site. Maybe I could visit a few days," asked Spring Flower.

"Do you think the others returning from rendezvous with you would like to come? Are they not at the entry of the valley, waiting for you?"

"No," she replied. "They are at the old camp and will be there for a while. They are still afraid to enter."

Annie stepped forward and said, "Of course you will come with us and stay as long as you would like."

On the trail, the women talked nonstop. I think that the girls really enjoyed hearing from the outside.

That evening after we had made camp, Spring Flower came to me saying, "This year, there were many more white men at rendezvous. There were many different tribes there also. The white men brought much more whiskey, and many Indians left with nothing.

"Two Mountains wanted to trade for whiskey, but I made our party leave before he could make any trade," she added.

"Do you want to stay here with us, in our valley?"

Spring Flower said, "If I stay, some of the party that went with me might let it be known where I am. There is much talk of your stallion. Many have spoken of wanting to ride a horse like that. If you ever brought him outside, they would probably steal him. Two Mountains told them you were going to breed horses. He told the braves that they would be able to trade for his offspring soon."

She added, "I would love to live here in this valley. Many days after we return to our camp, I will sneak away and come back here. Two Mountains tried to trade me for a jug of whiskey."

Over the next couple days, with Spring Flower's help, we got a lot of work done. When it came time to say good-bye, I had four crying women on my hands.

Spring Flower turned away, walking toward the entry to our valley, Knows Horses, hopping on a packhorse, raced to her side. "You will need this packhorse to return to us. We will be waiting."

I knew that it was my horse but Knows Horses seemed to always be thinking far ahead of me. And I had found out that, when you gave a present to these people, it could easily change your life.

CHAPTER THIRTEEN

We had finished our cabin and were stocking it with winter supplies. I had taught the three how to load and shoot their rifles. With their help, we had a good supply put up for winter. The horses were fat, and Knows Horses had them where she could walk up to them anywhere. The biggest part of the work was done, and now we spent a lot of time on the porch or exploring. Knows Horses had done a great job with the wild mares that Ollie had brought. They had fattened on the deep grass, and some were beginning to develop into good riding horses.

Susie, Knows Horses, and I were all riding the wild horses. We had gone out to check a mare that Knows Horses said was limping. She wanted to bring her to the corral to keep a close eye on her.

Ollie was coming to meet us when he stopped and looked back up the valley toward the entrance. When we got to where we could see what had caught his attention, we saw a rider about a mile off coming our way. We guessed that it was Spring Flower, since she'd said that she might return. We hurried to meet her. But as we got closer, we could tell it looked like a trapper. When we stopped before him, I noticed that it was one of the twins.

"What are you doing here?" I asked. "How did you find this place?"

He grinned and said, "An old Indian told me of this valley. For some of my whiskey, he told me of a beautiful buckskin stallion. He said a white man had him—that the man lived in this valley and it was full of beaver.

"Now I thought who else could it be but you and that horse of yours? I came to catch some of those beaver. I also intend to get my brother's horse that buckskin devil of yours carried off after he killed my brother."

The rage that overwhelmed me was about to take control of me. I knew this man had brought trouble for me. I knew that, if I was not able to handle him somehow, my family would be in great danger. This man was used to killing and taking what he wanted more than I had ever been. "You can turn around and leave," I told him firmly. "There is nothing for you here. If Ollie killed your brother, this world is a better place for everyone."

He had always been a man who tried to bully other people. He saw the three of us were armed. He kept looking at Knows Horses, sensing that he could be a dead man before long.

With a sneer on his face, he turned as if to leave. Then he decided to push a little farther. As he was turning, he said. "You owe me. I'll take that young squaw off your hands for payment."

The bullet knocked his cap off, but he was not stopping to pick it up.

I looked around. Susie was handing Knows Horses her rifle to reload. Then she was bringing Knows Horses rifle up to fire. I managed to stop her from firing again.

Knows Horses said, "We need to stop him."

"I do not want you killing anyone, unless they are trying to hurt us. And he is leaving fast."

I had given him a few days to clear out before I went to make sure he was gone.

When I found where he had camped, it looked as if he had left and brushed out his tracks. I decided to go toward the entry and see if I could find more signs of him.

There I found him. He had gotten to the entry, but had fallen from his horse. As I came closer, I saw he had three arrows in his back. Of the three arrows, two were Susie's. What was really strange was that one belonged to Annie.

The night before, Annie had sent me to the loft to sleep with Knows Horses. She and Susie had slept in the bed downstairs.

I decided to not say anything, except that he was long gone.

CHAPTER FOURTEEN

We were on the porch watching the shadows grow long. This might be the last evening before it would be too cold to sit outside. From the north, the snow clouds were beginning to roll in. We were stocked and ready.

Annie came and sat in my lap. She put her arm around me and said, "My husband, I have news for you. Before summer, you will have a child to follow you around."

I was so happy that I started to jump up, almost spilling Annie before I caught her. I pulled her close, and when the two other girls came close, we all hugged.

"You never give me a chance to be sad. I am always being surprised. This is the best surprise yet."

With the news, I begin to worry more about our safety. Although I had only seen danger come from the white man, I was sure that, sooner or later, the Ute warriors would find our valley.

I did not want to worry Annie with my thoughts. She was so happy about the baby coming. She and the other two were already preparing clothing. They had me build a little bed, and they filled it with the softest materials they could find.

One morning Annie had chosen to stay in bed. I explained to Susie and Knows Horses of my plans to make our home safer, lest we should be attacked.

"I want to remove anything around the cabin that an attacker can hide behind."

Knows Horses took her bow and shot an arrow as for as she could. "We will need to clear beyond the arrow. A strong warrior can shoot farther than I can."

"Will the Indians be able to get rifles?"

"I do not know. The white men are coming. They have guns. So, in time, yes."

We decided to clear as far as we could. Any time we were not busy with our chores, we would clear farther.

We made plans. If we were attacked, we would head to the cabin. We had it supplied for a siege. We had made it as strong as we knew how. Now we just had to have faith that things would work in our favor.

In late winter, Knows Horses came into the cabin after going out early to check on her mare. Her whole face was a smile. She was so excited she was having trouble telling us that her mare had given birth through the night. The colt looked exactly like Ollie.

Knows Horses was with the young colt about as much time as I had spent with Ollie. She had already begun to train it to follow her with a lead rope.

One morning, she led him out to where we had found the armor.

I had walked out to leave Annie in peace, for she said everyone was driving her crazy. I guessed we needed to give her some space.

I walked over to see what training Knows Horses had in store for the colt today. When I saw her, she was digging in the loose soil. She had pulled an old leather pouch out of the ground and was trying to hide it from me.

I did not mention that I had seen it. I wanted to see if she would explain what she had found. When she did not, I sat down as if I had not seen it.

"Do you remember the twin that we ran out of the valley?"

"Has he returned?" she asked.

"I doubt he can, with three arrows in his back."

"How long have you known?"

"I found him right before you and Susie took shovels back and buried him. I was in your bed. You did not leave the cabin. The arrows belonged to Annie and Susie."

She did not say anything. I sat there until the silence became a problem. She finally said, "Annie planned the whole thing and put the first arrow in his back. After we had told her what had happened, she knew he would not leave without bringing trouble. Annie knew he would go and bring back more men."

She went on to explain that Annie had sent Susie around to get his attention, with his back to her. Annie would then be able to get a few yards closer. Susie had gotten behind him and called his name. When he turned, he must have thought that the young squaw had come wanting trinkets.

Annie had been able to get close enough to put the arrow deep in his back. Susie had started to talk to him, but when Annie's arrow struck, he turned. Seeing Annie, he started to run for her. That was when Susie put her first arrow in him. He lay on the ground cursing them and telling what he was going to do with them. Susie walked up and put another arrow in his back, killing him.

They had put him on his horse and planned to turn him loose outside the valley. But then decided to come back and bury him instead. They pulled off the saddle and bridle. They hid them and released the horse. Susie and Knows Horses had gone back later and buried him. Annie had asked me to ride to the southern ridge to look around, so I would not know.

I sat for a while. My gentle Annie had done this.

"I cannot believe Annie has done this. It just doesn't seem to be in her nature."

Knows Horses asked, "Do you remember the day you took me for your wife? I told you not to expect us to be the same person.

"Annie is not going to let any threat come to our family. She starved herself to feed us. Annie is very kind, but you do not see everything."

I was sitting down, letting the story sink in. Knows Horses pulled the pouch out and threw it to me. I did not open it. I knew what it was.

"How much have you found?"

"Since we found the first stone, I have come back from time to time. I have found over twenty bags.

"I did not tell you about it because you will take it and buy things for us that we do not need. Others will see this gold and follow you back."

"I am going back to the cabin." I did not want to know where she was hiding the gold. "I will not follow you," I told her. "I will not come back here unless you invite me."

She came and pulled me close. "I will not withhold anything from you again," she said. "I have all you could give me here." She released me and removed her clothes and helped me with mine.

As I walked back to the cabin, I looked around at what we had— realizing that a mountain of gold could not make me any happier.

All around me was snow-capped mountains. Grass was waist deep and so green that it was almost blue. I had a fine home, three beautiful wives, and a child on the way. As far as I was concerned, the gold was useless.

CHAPTER FIFTEEN

This was the first spring in the new cabin, and the last snow had fallen. I had decided to go and check the other cabin and the pass. I wanted to look for any horse tracks that may have found their way in. If wild horses had found it before, more might return and bring trouble.

The women had packed plenty of provisions. I could get stranded and be unable to return. After the way Annie and her sisters had lost their parents, they made sure I had all that I would need.

When I walked out to get on my horse, Susie was sitting on hers. She had her rifle across her lap and her bow over her shoulder.

"You are surely a warrior woman."

"Is that my new name?"

"Is that what you want it to be? Do you like it?"

She smiled and said, "I will become your wife tonight."

Now I had kind of wondered when and how this was going to happen. Then I remember that Knows Horses had said it would come from the heart, and we would know when it was right.

We checked and found no sign that anyone had found our valley.

When we arrived at the cabin, it was just as it had been from the time we were last here. Warrior Woman went into the cabin to start a fire, while I tended the horses. When I came inside, the fire had warmed the cabin.

Warrior Women had laid our bed out in front of it. She was warming water for us to bathe. When the water was ready, she dropped her clothing and helped me with mine. She came to my arms and kissed me.

"I have waited, and my night is here."

As I kissed her, touching her body, she seemed to become so weak that I had to hold her up. We managed to pull apart long enough to take a bath. Then we were not apart again that night. We decided to stay a few more nights and enjoy ourselves, as I had done with my first two wives.

One night, we were lying in each other's arms. I asked, "If a warrior had placed a hide at your lodge, would you have thought of going with him?"

"Our whole life we knew it would be this way. But we did not expect it to be so good. The warriors of our tribe do not treat their women the way you have treated us.

"Each of us will fight to the death to protect our family."

We had checked the cabin, and now it was time to go home.

Annie and Knows Horses ran to Warrior Woman, chattering and laughing. I wondered if they were laughing at me. But they did not act as if they knew I was there.

Warrior Woman turned to me and said, "You have given me a new name. You should be the one to tell my sisters."

"From now on, Susie will be known as Warrior Woman."

I later thought about Annie's name. I had not yet given her a new name. She was my first wife.

When Annie and I were alone, I said, "It troubles me that I have never changed your name."

"When I became your wife, my name was Annie. You gave it to me, and I hope that it will always be my name."

That winter was uneventful. We mainly stayed in the cabin, unless I was out trapping. Annie grew bigger each day, and we were trying to do things for her without getting on her nerves.

CHAPTER SIXTEEN

This year, it seemed that spring would be coming early. The horses were feeding on tender spring grass. The wild geese were landing on the beaver ponds, and maybe soon we would be able to get out and start doing things.

We had eaten our meal and I had stepped out on the front porch when I saw the first rider.

It was a warrior, and it looked as if he was painted for war. I quickly stepped back in the cabin, closed the door, and opened my shooting hole. We had made notches in the wall so we could shoot from the inside. The women came to their spot and did the same. When I looked out, I could see that there were nine painted warriors, and they looked like they were ready for our scalps.

"When they charge, they will expect only one gun. Take aim from left to right," I instructed. "I will take the first shot. Then each of you follow, one at a time. They will not know how many guns we have."

If the war party did not see too many go down, they would continue to charge. After I shot first, I would have time to reload before the women had all shot, if they remained calm. If they shot true, I felt like we could get at least four of them and give me a chance to reload.

They came, and just like I had hoped, they came side by side. I knew that these warriors were serious about hurting us. They would kill me and take my wives as slaves. The horses would be rounded up and taken with them. If it was at all possible, they were fixing to learn that we were prepared.

I had the first one in my sights, and I rolled him off backward. The girls, seeing him go down, took their time and fired like we had planned.

I had reloaded and was preparing to fire again. There had been four lying dead or dying on the ground; now there were five.

They must have noticed that someone's medicine must be bad, given that the attack was not going in their favor. They turned to get out of range. I ran outside to try to get one more before they got too far.

Warrior Woman and Knows Horses came from the back side of the cabin. They had put the chest armor on and were riding to head the warriors off. I tried to call them back, but my two younger wives did not intend to let our attackers out of the valley.

If they got away, they would surely bring more back. I raised my gun, trying to get the last one. I fired but missed; he turned and charged me. I started to reload my rifle, but before I could get it loaded, he had gotten close enough to release an arrow. The arrow went just over my head. I took aim and put the sixth one on the ground. There were three more. I turned to get my horse and go after them, but Annie lay on the ground with an arrow through her chest.

I don't know how long I stood there trying to make sense of what I was looking at. It could not be Annie. I had left her inside, safe. We were winning, and she was going to be safe. I was pulling her into my arms and trying not to hurt her any more. I could see she was dying, and I could not do anything to stop it. I begged her not to leave me. She was not able to speak, but her eyes said it all. She would not be able to give me the child that we had all looked forward to. We would not be able to go on those overnight rides that she had come to enjoy. She would be unable to share the future we had all planned.

I had heard three shots spaced out, and I hoped they had been accurate.

I would learn later that Knows Horses and Warrior Woman had been able to get behind the warriors as they waited out of the range of our rifles. Knows Horses shot the first one, who looked to be their leader.

Before he hit the ground, the two remaining were circling, trying to decide which way to go. They thought they were surrounded. They attempted to make a dash for the pass, which was when Warrior Woman shot the second one from his horse.

Knows Horses and Warrior Woman stepped out in the clear so the last warrior would know that these women had stopped their attack. He strung his bow with an arrow but was blown from his horse when Warrior Woman got him in her sights.

I picked up Annie and carried her in the cabin. I could hear horses thundering close. I began to hear the two girls' war cries. At any other moment, their war cries would have been funny. But at this moment, my heart was torn from me.

As they came in the cabin, whooping and laughing, they saw the tragedy that had happened. Their laughter began tears of sorrow. We stayed there in our grief, trying to think what had gone wrong.

"I was being attacked. I had shot my rifle. I missed. I was trying to reload my gun. Annie must have seen I was not going to reload in time. She must have come out to protect me with her rifle. I did not know she was there. I am so sorry."

Knows Horses, through her tears, said, "Our Annie gave her life protecting her home. She chose a good way to die."

Warrior Woman asked, "Will you go dig the grave? We will wash and prepare her for burying."

I said, "She has always seemed to enjoy me bathing her, and I will do it for her one last time."

I buried her on a knoll behind the cabin, where every spring, flowers would bloom. It was a special place to her.

That night the three of us slept together and never said a word.

Weeks had passed. It was beginning to get hot, and I could not seem to get interested in doing anything.

I was sitting in the spot where Annie and I had shared many nights together. Knows Horses came and sit down and put her arms around me.

"Annie has left us. Do you remember the day you saw us carrying wood to our ragged tent? That night, we lay together thinking that you would be a great provider. But we thought we had no chance that you would choose us—our ragged teepee and three starving girls. Then we found your gift. Annie said the Great Spirit had come to her in a dream. The Great Spirit told her we would be happy with you.

"We have been happy. Now do you not know that you still have two wives—e two wives who miss you? Do not sit here and grieve so. Even Ollie seems to know that your spirit has died."

She got up and walked back to the cabin. I thought about what she had said and knew that she was right. But I felt like I was disrespecting Annie in some way.

I made up my mind to get up and start moving forward. The first thing I was going to do was to go see my oldest friend.

Ollie was standing there as if to say, *It is good to see you again.* I gave him a good rubdown. I looked at him and said, "Would you have ever believed that we would have ended up here, like this?"

He looked in my eyes as if to say, *We did all right.*

CHAPTER SEVENTEEN

It had been one year since we had lost Annie. I was beginning to get through a day without my heart breaking. I was allowing myself to remember the happy times that we shared.

I was standing out front one morning when I saw a rider coming. From this distance, I could not be sure, but it looked like Spring Flower. When she got close enough that I was sure, I let the girls know that we had company. They came out to meet her and were happy to have news from the outside.

Spring Flower had come to tell us that they were going to rendezvous. "Are you going to rendezvous this year?" she asked. "We will be leaving soon. We could travel together."

"I have not thought much about rendezvous this year," I told her. "Other things have happened."

Spring Flower asked, "Where is Annie?"

Knows Horses explained, "A war party came last year, after rendezvous. We had a battle. Annie was killed. We cannot understand how the war party was able to find our valley. But they do not live to tell others."

Spring Flower looked away for a while before turning and looking me in the eyes. "Last year at rendezvous, Two Mountains had been drinking with some Utes. It is possible that he traded information about the great stallion for whiskey."

Knows Horses asked, "May we go to rendezvous this year?"

I sit thinking about it. I really did not want to leave the valley unattended. If Two Mountains told the Utes, he would have told any tribe as long as he got whiskey. But maybe a change would do all of us some good.

"I guess we can go and do our own trading this year."

The girls were happy. We would trade our pelts and take the Indian ponies that we'd added to our herd. We would trade them for something of value.

We were loaded and moving through the pass when Warrior Woman asked, "Is Two Mountains going to be at rendezvous?"

Spring Flower said, "He will be there. He has all the pelts that I tanned for trade. I will have to watch him there, so he doesn't trade them for whiskey."

We made it to the old camp. The others from Spring Flower's tribe were waiting for us there.

Two Mountains came out, and you could tell that he had not expected to see us there. I was thinking at the point of getting down and trying to break his neck. But it was not in me to be violent.

I was looking in his guilty eyes when I heard the first arrow strike. Within seconds, the second arrow struck him in the chest. I did not have to look around to tell where they had come from. No one seemed to really care that my wives had just killed Two Mountains. It was more like they had expected it. His body lay where it landed. Everyone walked around him as they readied their packs to make the trip to rendezvous.

"How can you be so sure that it was him that was responsible for Annie's death?"

"We cannot be sure that he caused Annie's death. But he was the reason our parents died in the snowstorm. He left them in the storm. But he came back to the village, saying our parents were lost.' said Knows Horses. "When the weather cleared, Two Mountains went to hunt for them. He came back with our father's horse. If our parents had their horse, they would have been able to follow Two Mountains back. He left them to die, for a horse."

"When everyone realized what he had done, he became an outcast. After the younger warriors were killed by the Utes, he put himself in charge. He tried to regain his standing in the tribe. He did not help us to survive. He made us move our teepee from the rest of the camp. We lived on roots and berries. He did manage to get the tribe to safety, by using your horses. But we have never forgotten. Two Mountains killed our parents, and we knew this day would come," said Knows Horses.

The girls had never spoken of this.

I was beginning to understand more of their way of life. I had taught them how the white man lived. I had not asked much of their way of life. Unless I asked about something specific, they did not volunteer. It was like they would rather not talk about sad times.

CHAPTER EIGHTEEN

There were two families and Spring Flower who were traveling with us. The first family was a young warrior and his wife. The wife was Spring Flower's cousin. Her name was Morning Sun; the warrior was Black Elk. The other family was a young warrior that had taken Night Dove for a wife; his name was Many Kills.

Morning Sun and Night Dove had been riding double with their husbands. Knows Horses let them ride our horses, which she intended to trade. We would be able to get to rendezvous sooner, not having to stop to rest our horses.

The first night we camped, the two younger braves made a large loop around our camp. Black Elk returned, saying they had found no reason to worry about our location. After he had eaten, Black Elk went back out to keep watch. Soon Many Kills came in, had his meal, and then went back into the night. Each night they did this. We felt safe knowing they were out there.

After three days of traveling, we came to rendezvous. I had no idea they were so many white men in the mountains. I thought, *This is just the ones that came to rendezvous.* There was no way to tell how many white men had not come. Or how many white men had come and were already gone.

We made our camp out on the edge to stay away from the drunken trappers. Twice they came for Spring Flower—trying to trade for her favors. Black Elk and Many Kills sent them away, letting it be known that we had not come to trade our women.

I had traded my pelts for the things that Knows Horses and Warrior Woman wanted. I still had the three horses to trade.

Black Elk said, "I have talked to Many Kills, and we would like to trade for your horses. Night Dove and Morning Sun have talked of nothing else. They want horses, like your wives have."

Knows Horses said, "We want nothing else here. We will give your wives the horses as a gift. You have made us feel much safer on our trip. It is good that we can call you our friends."

Once again, Knows Horses had spoken for me.

Warrior Woman had joined in a shooting match with some young bucks. The young men did not want to shoot against her. But soon, the bystanders begin to call out to them. "What kind of warrior are you that you cannot beat a squaw?"

Then the match began in earnest. Warrior Woman did not beat the young bucks. But she was good enough to gain their respect.

As we walked and met new people, we gained news from the States. Some said the cavalry would be building new forts to protect the settlers moving this way. They would be hiring buffalo hunters to feed the troops. If a man had a way of getting beef to them, he would be able to make good money.

During our visit to Chief Gray Wolf's tribe, he asked, "Are you the woman known as Knows Horses? I have heard much of the horses you train. I am Gray Wolf, and no squaw can defeat me. I have a horse superior to anything that a squaw can train. I raided a Spaniard's camp in California and stole it from him. There is no horse his equal."

"I am Knows Horses, and my horse will beat your Spanish horse or any horse here. I say we will have a race and see how your Spaniard can run."

Knows Horses rode Ollie's first colt, Spirit, to the track. Races had already taken place; the ground had been torn up, but it was not muddy. This horse was her pride and joy. He looked just like Ollie, though he was not yet as big. She sat on Spirit, without saying a word. She stared at Gray Wolf,she knew she was intimidating the older man.

Gray Wolf looked annoyed with this woman. He would remove that bored look from her face. She had insulted him, saying she would beat his horse.

This white man did not know how to handle his woman. Perhaps after he won the race he would get a limb and teach this arrogant woman her place.

First he would win the race. He wanted to look at her face then. He would have two fine horses; he might take her also. He didn't want her, but it would please him to make her a slave.

Gray Wolf was talking loudly, giving people time to gather around before he disgraced this squaw.

"I will wager my horse against your horse. Do you, arrogant woman, wish to take your pony back and hook it to a travois? If you are afraid of losing this dog, I will understand."

I looked at Knows Horses, and she smiled. I was proud of her, more at that moment than ever before. She would make a statement. I was afraid that she might lose the horse that she loved. But she would not back down.

She looked at the chief. She showed her contempt for him. She acted as if he was a little boy who was going to learn a lesson. A man who would bet his prize possession was a fool and deserved to lose it.

By now, she had Gray Wolf so mad that I was afraid he might try and hurt her. I had my rifle ready, and I would kill him if he tried.

They moved to the starting line, and the chief left early. Knows Horses gave slack on the reins and did not let Spirit use up his energy. She let him work into those long strides. The track was about two miles in an oval shape. Spirit had not reached his top speed but was already gaining. After a mile she had caught up and took the lead. She was about fifty foot in front when she gave the horse free rein. Spirit started making those long strides faster and faster. He seemed as if he had a statement to make also. When Knows Horses crossed the finish line, she was one hundred yards in front.

Gray Wolf jumped from the horse and began to beat him with his quirt. The horse had run as hard as he could and was too winded to pull away from him.

Warrior Woman ran her horse into Gray Wolf, knocking him down.

When Gray Wolf jumped to his feet, Warrior Woman and Knows Horses had two arrows pointed at him.

Knows Horses said, "If you hit my horse again, I will kill you. It was not the horse's fault he lost. He had a fool for an owner."

Gray Wolf tried to make excuses. He said he had not bet his horse. The crowd he'd gathered to see him shame this woman would not let him lie his way out of his wager. He tried to stare her down. She just smiled at him. She was a woman who demanded respect.

Knows Horses took the reins from Gray Wolf and led her new horse away. The crowd was cheering her. I could tell from the way he looked at Knows Horses, we would have trouble from Gray Wolf. He had lost his prize possession and ability to brag, all to a squaw.

While Knows Horses rubbed her horses down, I asked, "Did you have to beat Gray Wolf that badly?"

"Gray Wolf's horse spoke to me, saying he wanted to come with us. So I had to make sure everyone knew who the winner was. There could be no doubt which horse was the greatest."

While the others finished with their trading, Knows Horses, Warrior Woman, and I walked around.

My wives had worn their finest clothing and left their hair hanging down their backs. They were the two most beautiful women there. I felt like trouble would be following us, but word of these women with bows over their shoulders must have gotten around.

We had grown weary and were ready to go home. We were returning to our camp to start packing for our return trip. That was when I heard my name called. It was a voice I'd hoped to never hear again.

I turned to stand face-to-face with Mathew Sparks and Pete Hayden. Mathew seemed to be unhappy with me for running out on them and said as much.

"I think you're just mad that you did not get Ollie," I retorted. "Maybe you are a little upset that you did not get to put that bullet in my back. Or was it you who shot me?"

"Pete took the shot, thought he missed."

I pulled up my shirt, showing my scar. Seeing the scar, he knew he had missed his chance when they had not followed me.

Mathew said, "You owe me a fee for bringing you to the mountains. It looks like you have done pretty good for yourself."

He made to put his hand on Warrior Woman's shoulder. She stepped back, and he was looking at the tip of Knows Horses's arrow. The look on his face was worth the trip. He had not expected these women to put up a fight. He thought that, because I had not fought in our old camp, he would have no trouble here.

Mathew stepped back and decided he would take another approach. "I mean no harm to the women, and I am still interested in buying Ollie."

"Ollie is not for sale; will never be. If you ever go near him, you will be scalped by these two women."

Mathew did not want to give up. I had gotten away with the prize he thought he should get. The twins must have left soon after I did. Without us there to do the work, things had not gone as planned.

Now I was seen as the envy of every trapper in the mountains. I had two beautiful wives and a fine breed of horses and plenty of pelts. I turned to leave, having nothing more to say to this man.

"I know about all that gold you have."

The three of us turned and asked, "What gold?"

"I made friends with a half-breed, part Spaniard and part Kickapoo. He told me of his grandpap going into a valley and bringing out gold the Spanish priest had been mining."

"They were using Indian labor to dig it from the ground. Some Spanish soldiers had gone to escort the priest and the gold to safety. They had been holding the Indians captive, using them for labor. When the Indians braves saw the soldiers go into the valley, they followed to rescue their brothers. As the story goes, no one ever came back out. I heard the place was watched over by evil spirits, but I don't believe in such.

"Last year, an old warrior, by the name of Two Mountains spoke highly of a buckskin stallion. He told me a white man had gone into that valley with such a horse. Now you are the only one that has a buckskin Stallion around here that I know of. And for a share of my whiskey, the old warrior told me where that valley was."

All this time, Pete stood with that toothless grin, not saying a word. But it looked as if he could smell gold and was ready to start spending.

As I turned to leave, Knows Horses was notching an arrow.

"You cannot do this here," I told her. "They will not let you get away with killing a white man."

"If we let him get away, he will surely follow. He will bring more men."

"We will have to wait, watch for him. Maybe he will follow. We can get him on the trail."

She was not happy. "I have him now. Let me kill him. You escape with Warrior Woman."

I pulled her close, saying, "I will not lose another part of my life. We must prepare to leave now."

We spoke to Black Elk and Many Kills of what had happened, telling them we would leave now.

"If you want to stay longer, do so. But keep an eye on Mathew and Pete," I cautioned. "They might try to follow behind us."

Black Elk said, "We will finish trading and watch for these men. If they do not follow in a day's time, we will leave and catch up with you on the trail."

Knows Horses said, "You know they will come."

"We must stay prepared, but maybe Black Elk and Many Kills will take care of our problem."

Warrior Woman had not said a word. We were well on our way when she asked, "What is this gold that he was talking about?"

Over the years, Knows Horses and I had never spoken of the gold she'd found, and Warrior Woman had never been told of it. After we explained what gold was and that we had found it in our valley and what evil men would do to get it, she agreed that it should not be spoken of. But apparently it was too late. Two Mountains and whiskey had betrayed us.

Before we stopped for the night, a rider, coming fast, was behind us. It was Spring Flower. In our haste to leave, we had forgotten about her.

"You told me once that, if I needed someone to care for me, I should come to you. May I now come and live in your valley with you? With Two Mountains dead, I have no one to help me."

I looked at my wives for an answer. I wanted to help her as I had promised, but I would prefer for them to make the decision.

Knows Horses said, "After we killed Two Mountains, I had planned to ask you to come with us. But I did not know that we would leave so soon."

It was settled. Spring Flower would move into Annie's cabin. Knows Horses said that I would come and teach her how to shoot Annie's rifle. They would help her make a good bow and some arrows. Using the bow would save ammunition and would not signal our location.

On the third day, Black Elk and Many Kills came to our camp late in the evening. Black Elk and Many Kills said that Mathew had left with two other men. But they did not follow our trail.

Black Elk said that Gray Wolf had made much talk about Knows Horses—what he would teach her, when he saw her again. The people said that Knows Horses had whipped him bad the first time. She would show no pity the next time. He would not be able to live in his shame and would come one day.

CHAPTER NINETEEN

I felt better knowing that, at this time, no one was on our trail, and I was ready to get to our little cabin. We would watch for Gray Wolf, for he would surely come. Until he could dance with Knows Horses's scalp around the fire, this would not be over. I felt certain that Mathew would find men who, like him, would be willing to kill for gold, and they would come.

I wanted to get busy building something but had no idea as to what. Then it hit me; it was not that I wanted to build anything in particular. I missed working with Knows Horses, Warrior Woman bringing us food and water, the three of us taking long breaks together. At times, we would just lie in the shade and take naps. We'd had happy times before Annie's death, and it was time to get back to enjoying our lives. I thought of the trappers—in freezing weather, trying to get enough pelts just so they could get drunk next summer. I was a rich man. Fate had given me a great life, and I would enjoy everything.

Spring Flower had moved into Annie's cabin. The wives were helping her with her bow. They shot arrows until her arm was strong enough to bring down a deer. I was teaching her to load the rifle. I had been teaching her to aim it without firing. I wanted her to know how to operate the gun well before she fired. We would not fire the gun much. The noise would travel far and give away our position. You never knew who was outside our valley.

The evening before she returned to her cabin I was showing her how to hold the rifle. "When you fire it, if you do not hold it tight to your shoulder, it will cause severe pain," I explained.

Spring Flower had been easy to teach, but there was a difference in her. When she had found me, alone and wounded, she had taken charge. She had known what needed to be done; she had given the orders, and they had been followed. Now she seemed to just accept her fate. She had a sadness to her.

"Are you not happy here?" I asked. "Is there something wrong?"

At first she said nothing, and then tears formed in her eyes. She turned to me and asked, "Will I ever be your wife?"

I remembered what she had been to me. I remembered the sad look on her face the morning I had left her camp. Not knowing what leaving my hides at a different lodge meant. Not knowing her customs. Not knowing that our having stayed in a lodge together meant that she could have already been my wife.

"I will talk to Knows Horses and Warrior Woman."

When I started the discussion with Knows Horses and Warrior Woman about Spring Flower, Warrior Woman asked, "Do you want another wife?"

"Not really. But I feel like I owe her," I explained.

"Wait till your heart speaks," she answered.

I decided that I would not think about another wife. Spring Flower was here with us. She had a good cabin, food to eat, and was as safe as we could make her. Whatever happened need not be rushed.

There were nine mares, with the two that we had taken from the Ute war party. We had four colts from Ollie, and Knows Horses was busy with them. She was training them and did not want anyone around. She wanted the colts' full attention.

I had walked to the corral to see how things were coming. The past few days, Knows Horses had not been herself. She usually had input on whatever we were talking about. But the last few days, she had been quiet.

"How are the colts coming along?"

"We should get a good price for Ollie's four next year."

She seemed as though she wanted to be left alone. I crossed the rail fence and pulled her to me and asked, "Do you remember me?"

75

She lay her head on my shoulder and began to cry. After a while, I led her to a bench under the shade tree. Knows Horses does not cry. This was a first, and I waited. I did not want to say anything that might make it worse.

"I do not want you to throw me away."

"Why would I want to get rid of my wife? I won't ever let you go."

"When a warrior's wife cannot have a child, he can throw her away. He can get another wife to have children—to make sure the tribe will stay strong."

"If you get with child, I would be happy. But if you do not, it would make no difference to me. I will not throw you away."

"I have been with child twice and lost both."

"I am sorry you did not tell me you were with child. Next time, let me know. Warrior Woman and I will do more of your work. But child or not, you will always be my wife."

Spring Flower had been with us for two years, and we traveled from cabin to cabin helping each other.

I was planning a trip and asked Warrior Woman to come.

Knows Horses said, "You need to go alone. It is time that you gave Spring Flower a child."

"I have not given either one of you a child. What makes you think I can give Spring Flower one?"

"We will not know unless you try."

I made many trips, and we did try. That winter, she got with child.

Knows Horses brought her to our home and would not allow her to do any work. The women took care of Spring Flower as if she were a baby.

CHAPTER TWENTY

It was the early part of May. I had ridden to the pass to look for any new tracks. I turned up the trail that led up to the old cabin. There they were, five sets of tracks. All shod horses. White men.

I turned, heading back to our cabin. We needed to get prepared.

I told the women, "I found shod tracks of five men. They are at Spring Flower's cabin. They will try to catch us separated and then attack. We will face rifles this time."

For a week, we stayed in the cabin or very close, always being careful.

A little after daylight a week later, we were having our meal. Mathew Sparks called out. He was just out of my range, but he had a white flag.

Knows Horses said, "I will not let him come close."

"Let him come. While he is talking, watch for the others. They will be getting in position—trying to pen us down."

She moved Spring Flower back away from the openings. Knows Horses then went to the back of the cabin so she could watch for movement. She had a clear view behind the cabin.

Mathew came slowly—too slowly, giving his men time to surround the cabin.

"Zack, you have three choices. You can tell us where the gold is. We will take it and leave. You can take your squaws and leave. You can try to fight, and we will kill you. We will have the women, the horses, and the gold. There are five of us, and you don't stand a chance. Take your pick now."

I started to say we would fight when Knows Horses's gun exploded. She had Pete in her sites all the time.

When the gun went off, Mathew turned his horse, holding up his flag, saying, "Don't shoot. I came peaceful."

Warrior Woman cut loose on him. His shirt was soaked with blood before he hit the ground.

I looked at Warrior Woman, "What are you doing?"

In her typical humorous way, she said, "Were you not through talking?"

I could hear Knows Horses as she left the cabin. Her horse was headed out to circle behind them. I had told them to stay in the cabin, but she did not intend these men to leave the valley.

Warrior Woman went to Spring Flower and said, "Do not leave the cabin."

As she stepped out, headed for her horse, I said, "You are not going. Stay with Spring Flower. I will help Knows Horses."

She pointed toward Spring Flower and said, "She carries your child. If you are killed, who will raise him?"

Without another word, she was on her horse and gone. I tried to give her rifle cover, but she was out of their range.

One of the men had taken cover, closer than I had thought, and he took a shot at me. But the shot fell short.

I went to Spring Flower to calm her. She was afraid Knows Horses and Warrior Woman would not return. I explained to her that I would hate to be any of those men. They had made the mistake of underestimating my wives. They would die before this day ended. She seemed to calm down, and I went to the door and stepped just outside.

The man who had shot at me stood just out of rifle range, with a flag of truce waving. He knew he had been left alone. He had seen my wives going after his pals. He realized he could not join his friends without having to pass Knows Horses or Warrior Woman to get to them.

I told him, "Put the gun down and come closer."

When he was close, I could see it was the other twin. I had started to ask him wasn't he supposed to be dead when a shot rang out. From the direction it came, I knew he probably had lost another partner.

"Now there is just two of you," I told him. "You can go look if you want to."

He looked as if he might want to go help his partners but decided to take his chances with the flag. Another shot rang out.

"All we need to do now is decide what to do with you."

His knees begin to shake, and I thought he would be sick.

He managed to say, "I give up. I have a flag of truce. You can't shoot me with this flag."

I could hear the horses returning. My wives were whooping and hollering like wild warriors. They skidded to a stop and dismounted.

"Why is he still alive?" they asked together.

"His brother had said that Ollie killed him, but here he is. I told him we would decide what to do with him."

Knows Horses said, "You will be allowed to run to this arrow." She released it, and the arrow landed about one hundred yards from where we stood. "When you reach my arrow, you are a dead man."

He started crying and showing his flag.

"You have two choices. Die here crying like a woman or run like a man." He ran as fast as he could run, instead of saving his energy. When he got to the arrow, he was too tired to run fast.

Knows Horses dropped him with her rifle.

We drug the bodies deep into the woods, where the stink would not bother us.

The buzzards would pick their bones clean.

I knew not to say anything about the battle. Twice my wives had fought, and I could do no better.

Warrior Woman and I went to the loft bed that night. When we were settled in bed, she began to talk about the battle. She told me that, when she straddled her horse, going to join Knows Horses, she had such a rush. She wanted to get there before Knows Horses had a chance to kill the men.

"Is this what warriors feel when they go into battle? I have never felt this feeling before. I felt no fear."

"How were you able to kill them?" I asked.

"When I got to Knows Horses, she pointed to one of the men hiding in rocks beside the stream. Knows Horses said he was too far off for her to make an accurate shot."

Warrior Woman said, "I walked out and showed myself with only my bow. When he saw my bow, he worked closer for a better shot or maybe try to take me hostage.

"Knows Horses did not show herself. She waited until he was in her range and took the shot that sent him to the happy hunting ground."

The second man had hidden in a grove of timber. He had seen Warrior Woman and was easing up behind her when Knows Horses made her shot, killing the first one. He did not know how many people were in the forest. He turned to run; he was so afraid he tripped. He stood with his hands up in surrender and Knows Horses killed him.

"Why were you standing in the open? Did you not realize there might have been one behind you?"

"At the time I was so excited. All I thought of was how I would make love to you tonight."

She did. She was so wild I thought she might scalp me. The next morning, she looked as if she was embarrassed and left the loft early.

CHAPTER TWENTY-ONE

Warrior Woman stayed to herself for a couple days. I did not bother her. I would let her work out whatever it was she was going through. At the end of the second day, she was at Annie's grave, and I approached her.

"Come and sit, I have been thinking about how I acted. I feel I have gone to far with our lovemaking. I am sorry."

"Warrior Woman, if you feel that way after going into battle, I might have to let more men know about the gold."

We both had a good laugh, and life was back to normal.

The rest of the summer went well.

Knows Horses had decided not to trade the colts this year. She thought that, in another year, they would be worth double. We decided not to go to rendezvous. So we had picnics and entertained Spring Flower.

We had taken some of our skins and built a teepee. We spent many nights with a campfire, and the women danced as the warriors had done when they lived with their tribe.

November came storming. The snow came, and it turned very cold. We worried about the horses. On cold days, they would run up and down the valley, kicking up their heels. They seemed as prepared for winter as we were.

One night after Knows Horses and I checked our herd, the moon was coming up over the cliffs of the canyon. I can't remember it every being that large and bright. The whole valley lit up almost as clear as day. We were standing there just looking at it when Warrior Woman came to the door and said, "Spring Flower's time has come."

It was a long night, and though Spring Flower was in much pain, she never made a sound. We had piled in bed alongside her. When her pains eased, we talked about nothing in general, just helping her pass the time.

Knows Horse called me outside. "Warrior Woman and I wonder why you have not made Spring Flower your wife yet?"

"I have been waiting for my heart to speak."

Knows Horses looked me in the eye. She had a look that she used when she wanted to get a point across. "And?"

I knew that my mind had been made up for me.

I knew what I had to do. I asked Knows Horses and Warrior Woman to step out for a while. I went to Spring Flower, and in between pains, I asked, "Will you be my wife?"

"If I die giving you this child, I will be happier than I have ever dreamed. You have given me a family that cares for me. If I live to be old, I know I will not die alone."

Just about an hour before the sun came up, Spring Flower gave us a baby boy.

As I held him I said, "We will call him Big Moon, and his English name would be David Morris."

CHAPTER TWENTY-TWO

Through the winter, I was able to take some fine pelts. The cold, frigid temperature had caused the beaver skins to be extra thick.

The baby was growing and always had someone to tend to his needs.

On a cold winter night, Knows Horses and Warrior Woman had both come to my bed in the loft.

Warrior Woman said, "I have good news. What I have waited on so long has happened. I am with child."

We were happy. Both Knows Horses and Warrior Woman were crying. I kissed her long, holding her close.

I knew Knows Horses was glad when she heard the news. But I knew this was the same news she wished she could share one day. She had carried two children but had had no child. I released Warrior Woman and said to Knows Horses, "When the time is right, it will happen to you."

She squeezed me close and said, "Don't leave me tonight."

I felt a little embarrassed to ask Warrior Woman to leave the loft. I think she understood, for she came and hugged and kissed us both.

Winter became spring and still Knows Horses had no news to share.

The sun had moved closer to summer when I saw Black Elk and Many Kills come slowly to our cabin. As they came up, they were looking at the horses Knows Horses had in the corral.

"Come, sit. Will you eat with us?"

Knows Horses came and spoke to them.

She said, "They have come to see the great stallion they have heard about." Knows Horses whistled.

It was not long before Ollie came thundering up to her.

The two warriors stood with mouths open. They were unable to speak. They could only look at the greatest horse they had ever seen.

Knows Horses spoke with them as Warrior Woman and Spring Flower brought them food. She spoke to Ollie, and he returned to the herd.

I asked, "What are they talking about?"

Knows Horses said, "They want to know what it would take to own such a horse. I told them they would never own him. But if they have something of value, they might trade for his colts. They are broke and ready. I told them to remember the colt who won the race at rendezvous."

Many Kills said, "We have Spanish cattle outside our valley. We will trade them for the four colts in the corral."

"How many cattle?"

"We have eight cows and one bull."

"We will look at them before we talk trade."

After we had eaten, Knows Horses led four of the young horses out.

Black Elk, Many Kills, Knows Horses, and I rode out to look at the cattle. While we rode, Knows Horses asked the warriors, "Why are you not afraid to enter the valley?"

"Spring Flower told us, if we came in peace, the spirits would not harm us. The great stallion has gained favor with the Great Spirit. He guards the valley."

Once we left the entrance to our valley, we turned north up the canyon. We traveled about two miles. There was a small box canyon to the east. The Indians had driven the cattle into the canyon and built a wall of brush to hold them until they returned.

The cattle were grazing, and we got a good look at them. They looked to be thin and hungry. Some had ribs showing. There were two calves, about three hundred pounds each. The braves had not mentioned them.

Knows Horses said, "I will trade two horses for all the cattle."

The two braves did not want to leave with only two horses. But they did not want to leave without any of this bloodline.

Knows Horses had gotten the young horses for the trip. She wanted the warriors to get a taste of some of the finest horseflesh they would ever ride. She knew that, after riding these horses, they would not leave without them.

"I will give the horse I won from Gray Wolf for the two calves."

"It is a trade," said Many Kills.

We removed the wall of brush and drove the cattle into the valley. When they reached the cabin, they went straight to the grass and began to graze.

The horses came to check out the cattle. Ollie circled them a couple times and took his herd and went back to the northern end of the canyon.

The cattle started to graze in the opposite direction. They must have come to an understanding, for they did not fight and did not mix.

CHAPTER TWENTY-THREE

We had our home, and we had plenty of wild game. We had our cattle, we had the finest horses in the West, and we had each other. I often thought, *What would I have done, had I chosen not to leave Mississippi after my parents died?*

What if Mathew Sparks had not come to me in St. Louis wanting to buy Ollie? What if they had not been planning to kill me if they could not get him any other way? Things always seem to have been preplanned. I did not understand it, but I knew that I could never have done as well on my own. I thought back, and almost everything that happened was because I did not really know what I was doing. Maybe my parents and Annie were watching over us.

Knows Horses was sitting in the swing I had built under the shade of the porch.

I fixed her a cup of coffee so we could relax and drink it in the shade. I was talking with her about adding a porch on the back of the house.

Knows Horses's mind was far away. She had not heard a word that I had said.

She looked at me, saying, "Let's go on the buffalo hunt with my people. We have not had buffalo meat in years. I would like to go with the tribe once again. There was so much happiness when the kill was made. The feast and the dancing at night, visiting with old friends and family, preparing the meat for winter use—I miss it. I would love to go again before it is too late. Moon is big enough to go, and Warrior Woman can still ride."

I had not wanted to leave the valley, but I thought it would do us good to get out from time to time. There was nothing holding us now. The ones who had found their way into our valley were dead. We would go.

Knows Horses jumped up and ran in to the cabin. You could hear the women outside as Knows Horses told the news. They were happy. You could hear it in their voices. This was a part of their lives that I knew little about. I felt I needed to experience it with them.

Knows Horses and I rode out the next morning to find the tribe and see when they would be leaving.

Black Elk said that scouts were out now watching for the herd—that we should be ready to go as soon as word came in that the herd was near.

We returned immediately, packed our tepee, and gathered supplies. We picked our best horses for riding and loaded our packs on the pack horses.

We would be gone from our valley for a while, and we hoped it would be safe.

When we got back to the tribe and set up our tepee, it reminded me of when I had first met these people.

Things had changed much since then. The people were not starving, and there were plenty young braves around to provide protection.

At night, the fire was the gathering place. The warriors danced into the night for a good hunt. As I sit and watched my wives enjoying the visit, I wondered why we had waited so long to come and spend time together.

The following day, one of the scouts returned; the herd was getting close. So far, they had not been followed by another tribe. We began to break camp and were on the trail. Some of the children were on horses with the women who had horses. The rest walked alongside. It was a happy time; you could see it in the faces of the group. We were strung out in a line a quarter mile long. We were going over the pass that Spring Flower had brought me over years ago.

We reached the plains and set up camp near a stream. We were back in the rocks and brush far enough to not draw attention.

The men made the plans. Knows Horses would not be allowed to go, and she seemed to understand. I was allowed but had to stay with Black Elk.

We had stopped where we could look over the herd. It looked like a giant black mass sliding along over the grass. I had seen large herds before but nothing like this. I doubted that I would live long enough to count all of them if I tried.

We would not try and attack this large body. We would wait. Many would come to the stream close by. They had picked a spot where, over the years, the buffalo had come to water, and then they would rest in the shades along the stream.

Black Elk had found a tall rock that I was supposed to lay on where I could get a good shot. The braves would circle around and drive a smaller bunch away from the large herd, hoping not to disturb the other buffalo. If the hunt failed, we would not have to travel far to catch back up with the rest of the herd. I had two rifles loaded and lying beside me as the herd passed. I was to shoot and kill as many as I could.

They had waited until about one hundred animals had come to water. I was watching the big herd when the smaller bunch came in my direction.

The hunters were riding behind and beside them. I saw a cow go down and realized it was fixing to be my turn. I could not imagine riding a horse in that mass. The warriors would get close enough to the buffalo that they could touch them. If they fell off, they would be trampled to death. I could not believe how they could hang on with their legs and shoot the buffalo at the same time. I raised my rifle and dropped a bull. Before he hit the ground, I grabbed my second rifle and shot a large fat calf before reloading. The buffalo were about to get too far away. I was able to drop another bull; it was just about out of my range. Through the dust, I could see the warriors start to break off the hunt.

The hunters had killed all they could.

The buffalo that had not been shot began to slow and return to the big herd. It was as if they had forgotten the mad dash to get away. The main herd seemed to not notice what was going on and kept grazing along.

Knows Horses and Spring Flower, with Moon, joined me at the side of the young calf. It would be some good tender meat. The women begin to cut it up in small bundles so we could handle the heavy weight.

Moon was given a piece of the heart. He had blood all over his face and seemed to love it. They offered me the rest. I turned it down. Knows Horses and Spring Flower shared it, as they probably had done many times before. I still had to have my meat cooked. The women would laugh at me, but that was the way it was. I had never eaten raw meat and was not fixing to change.

Black Elk asked about the other two kills I had made.

"We have plenty. Give them as presents."

We needed to make sure that everyone had all they needed for the winter. The tribe would not touch a buffalo without the hunter that had made the kill's permission.

When I looked around, everyone was cutting up meat. I knew it was important; the tribe had to get all the meat they could to get them through the long winter. I thought about how long they had done this, long before I had come west, and about how many white men had joined in a hunt with them. I was going to ask Black Elk how they had killed the giant beasts before they'd had horses. How had they gotten close enough for a kill?

Knows Horses had built our fire large and was cooking much meat.

She said, "My husband will share his kill tonight." It was not long before the ones who were just finishing butchering their kill came through. Knows Horses told them to eat from our fire.

Everyone was too tired to dance around the fire that night. They were thankful to the ones who had cooked for them. Knows Horses, Warrior Woman, and Spring Flower had cut up and cooked steaks for the ones with teeth and boiled stew for the elders. The older ones preferred the fat and would swallow large pieces. I had eaten so much I could not see me eating again for a week.

I was sitting on the backrest Knows Horses and Warrior Woman had made for me when they started to braid my hair. They had never done this before.

"Why would you want to do this?"

Warrior Woman said, "When you first came to us, we were very poor. We want to show off our husband who has given us so much. The women in this camp who were mean to us now envy us. They see us as very favored because of the horses that we ride and the many fine clothes we wear."

Later, they paraded me around the camp. They made sure everyone remembered the night I had given them the skins. They talked of the great stallion, our home, and the cattle we had traded for.

Spring Flower had been watching Moon play with his new friends. At first he was frightened, but he'd joined them, not showing his fear. Spring

Flower was worn out with all his wandering. When she came to us, you could see the pride in her eyes.

We walked around and spoke to everyone and then went to our teepee. It had been a long day, and we needed to rest. Tomorrow the tribe would smoke and dry meat. The day after, we would hunt again.

I was sitting on my backrest next to the fire. Black Elk and Many Kills stopped and sat down. I asked them, "How did you kill the buffalo before you had horses?"

Many Kills said, "The old ones would cover themselves with buffalo hides and ease close enough to cut the tendons in the buffalo's legs. Then they would not be able to walk. The buffalo would see the warriors in the hides but would not be afraid.

"Some ran the buffalo over the cliffs, but that wasted many animals," he added. "The Great Spirit was not happy. The Great Spirit saw all the waste and sent us the horse. The horse has allowed us to have much warmer teepees, plenty of meat, and plenty of warm clothes. With the horse, we are able to follow the herd longer. Before, we did not eat much buffalo meat and built shelters any way we could."

While living with the tribe, I had noticed that what Knows Horses had told me about the men was correct. Their first love was stealing horses; the second was going to battle. The third was horse racing; the fourth was gambling. The fifth was women. The woman was a possession that was more of a slave than a wife.

During the day, other warriors had come and talked with me. Most wanted to talk of the great stallion that I had. They wanted to know if we had any more of his young to trade.

"You will have to talk to Knows Horses. She trains them, and she will decide when it is time to trade."

The men acted as if it was beneath them to trade with a woman. They were willing to pay great amounts for the horses but could not believe that I would leave such an important matter to a squaw.

The next day, the herd was getting close to passing us. We planned our last hunt. It would be the same as before, but Knows Horses would be with me. The braves had decided that she could reload my rifles so we could kill more buffalo.

The buffalo was circled again, and they came close. As fast as I shot,

Knows Horses took my gun and reloaded it. On the fourth shot, she took it herself and dropped a fat cow. She was more excited than when she and her sister had killed Matthew and his men.

The hunters followed the herd longer this time, making sure that we would be well supplied.

Again my wives cut up the young buffalo and started cooking for the camp. Since we had more meat to butcher this hunt, the women of the camp would work long into the night. It would be late before we were able to eat. But by cooking, my wives ensured the people were fed and were happy. They had made life a little easier for the tribe.

The next morning found everyone busy. Buffalo hides were stretched everywhere you looked. Meat was being dried, and each fire had a cooking pot boiling. If we could make the trip home without anyone being hurt, it would be a huge success.

The elders were discussing where to winter. Some wanted to go north and join another band and attack the Arapaho in the spring. Most wanted to make the trip back, where there was plenty firewood. When the decision was made, they chose to return to the place where we had found them. It would allow us to join them for the spring hunt.

I had watched the men race their horses, but none would race Knows Horses and Spirit.

If we stayed much longer, it would be hard for Moon to leave his new friends. We had enjoyed our visit, and I was able to see the tribe when life was much better. The women wanted to stay longer, but I was worried about our home. We had been gone for almost three weeks. I had really enjoyed their life; it was so simple. Where our lives would be confined to our valley, they were free to change locations when they chose.

CHAPTER TWENTY-FOUR

Late fall, just before the first snow fell, my little Annie was born. Warrior Woman had wanted to name her daughter for her sister, and everyone agreed. She was a beautiful little girl and seemed to always be happy. You never heard her cry. Knows Horses seemed to lose her desire to take charge. She had a way of just letting things happen. I knew that she wanted to have a child. But until it happened, I knew of no way to help her.

Moon had really loved visiting his cousin Little Cougar and his other friends. Although his friends treated him as a white man, they still let him go on hunts with them.

Spring Flower had always tried to keep him as close as possible. She did not understand that he needed young men his own age to be with. After waiting so long to have a child, she overprotected him.

Moon was a loving child, but he needed to go into the world—to see what else was there. He had learned to trap with me and helped with the horses. He missed his friends and the life they lived.

It was early January 1850. Warrior Woman, Spring Flower, and Annie were in their room discussing clothes. Annie was growing out of most of what she had.

Knows Horses and I were in the large room where the family all gathered. Knows Horses said, "We need to talk."

I said, "I can tell you have something bothering you. What is it?"

She said, "Moon is going hunting with his cousins. He is staying with them more and more. I am afraid that, one day, he will not return. Spring Flower will not be able to handle him gone. If he takes the warriors' trail, he could be killed."

"Yes, I have seen a change in him. At sixteen, he is considered a man among the warriors."

"I have one more thing to talk about," she added. "The spirits have smiled on me. I am with child."

How many questions can a brain come up with before you pick out the right one? I could not get answers fast enough. I had never expected it to happen after she had lost two.

"I have carried this baby two months, a month longer than any other. I was afraid I would lose it, but I feel it is safe to tell you now."

The next morning, we all sat down and made new laws. The others would do her work, and Knows Horses would no longer work with the horses. She would not be able to enjoy the active life she had known. To our amazement, she agreed.

Knows Horses and Warrior Woman had decided it would be best to send Annie, who had turned fifteen, to the white man's school. The white man was coming and bringing their families.

Annie would probably be the only one left to tend the valley. Moon was spending more of his time with his friends and did not care for the valley. She would need their education to survive. Without schooling, when the white people came into this valley, she would know nothing of their culture.

I agreed, but we would wait two more years. This had been weighing heavy on my mind. We had been protected over the years, but things were changing rapidly.

Moon was spending more and more time with his cousins. Each time he left, he came back with anger. I could see he was building up more hatred for the white man. We had tried to explain that change was coming—that the old ways would disappear. Spring Flower had begged him to follow the white man's trail. I tried to get him to go with me on trips, to see the cities so he could judge for himself and to see that the old ways were all but gone. I had talked to him about school, but he wanted nothing to do with the white man's school.

He'd left in early spring and had not returned. We heard talk from the outside of skirmishes with other tribes and even a few fights with the cavalry. But so far, no word had come of Moon's band attacking the army.

CHAPTER TWENTY-FIVE

In Early August, Knows Horses gave birth to a beautiful little girl.

"I will name her Elizabeth Morris," she announced. "I have always loved the name, and I believe it will bring my daughter as much happiness as it has me. It was the first name you gave me, and I have never forgotten it."

Smiling, I said, "It is a perfect name. She will bring us much joy."

Annie was ever present, tending to Beth—just as my Annie had taken care of her sisters. Time was flying; we were busy and happy with our lives.

Beth was two years old now. Annie was preparing to go away to school. Warrior Woman and I would be traveling with her. We would be gone a long time from this valley. We planned to stay until we felt she was adjusted and safe.

Knows Horses had retrieved two sacks of gold and insisted that we take it for our expenses. We would not be able to trade horses for her education.

Arriving in St. Louis, we went to the nearest bank with the gold. We had no idea of its value.

Warrior Woman explained, "We are here for our child's education. We would like to deposit our gold so we can use it while we are in St. Louis." We had made up a lie and told the teller we were looking at the banks to see who would give us the best deal.

The teller who waited on us was William Peterson.

He asked, "Did you bring this gold all the way from California? I can assure you, I will give you the best price for your gold. And I will invest it where it will continue to grow.

"I will deposit the money in an account for your daughter," he explained. "She will be able to draw from it as she needs money."

We were to enroll Annie and then find a boarding house and report back with the expense. Mr. Peterson would give her a budget to go by. As long as she stayed with the budget, her money would never run out.

Warrior Woman and I decided that we needed to learn as much about money and banking as we could while we were here.

With us settled in, we begin to look around. Warrior Woman and Annie looked more like sisters than mother and daughter. Young men were falling over themselves to wait on them. I had really expected them to avoid us, but my wife and daughter's beauty seemed to demand respect.

Annie had been taught as much as I was able to teach her. She was taught how to pay attention and remember everything by Warrior Woman. Annie had grown up with adults and was for more experienced in surviving than most young women of her age. Who were only interested in parties and friends.

In school, she excelled. She became popular with the kids her age. She was being invited to all the parties. Wherever she went, there was always a crowd.

CHAPTER TWENTY-SIX

Knows Horses and Spring Flower had enjoyed the early spring. They had been tempted to join the tribe and go hunting. But they were afraid that Warrior Woman and I might return and be worried.

Knows Horses was riding one of Ollie's offspring with Beth. They had been out looking for more of the gold. Beth loved to ride the horses with her mother and seemed to have that knowledge that Knows Horses possessed.

Knows Horses was beginning to work her way up the stream that she and Zack had bathed in so long ago. As she looked back across to the cabin, there was a man leading two burros. He seemed to be heading toward the cabin.

She made her way to the cabin, where Spring Flower was alone. She may not be aware that someone was coming. Knows Horses arrived just as Spring Flower stepped out of the cabin and looked in the direction of the intruder.

Knows Horses, with only her bow for protection, handed Beth to Spring Flower. She would give him a chance to explain what business had brought him. She felt like she should go ahead and kill him, not giving him a chance to overpower them.

The old prospector did not know if the women he faced spoke English. Surely there must be a white man around somewhere from the looks of the cabin and other things that white men used. The woman on the horse had removed her bow. The look on her face let him know he was walking on eggshells. He had begun to think he had made a mistake. He would mind his manners and try to leave if possible.

The woman with the bow strung an arrow and asked his name.

"I am Samuel Burks. People call me Sam. I came in the valley looking for gold and saw the cabin. I did not know anyone lived here. After I saw the cabin, I started to leave. I just felt like I should let you know that I meant no harm."

Knows Horses asked, "How many men are with you?"

Sam said, "I am alone, except for my burros. I was searching for gold when I found the entrance. I am on my way to California. I decided to look and see if I was passing up gold on the way."

Knows Horses said, "We do not let people enter and roam in this valley. This is our home."

He asked, "Can I go back to the stream and camp tonight? I will leave the next day."

Knows Horses said, "You will sleep on the porch. Tomorrow I will escort you out."

Sam did not sleep very well that night. The woman with the bow acted like she would put an arrow in him. And it would be no different to her than killing a fly. Several times through the night, he knew she checked to see if he was still there. As bad as he needed to empty his bladder, he would not move.

The next morning, the women seemed pleasant enough and fed him. As he was loading his burros, Knows Horses talked to him a little more. It was as if she wanted to know something. He felt that, before he left, she would find a way to ask.

Ollie was close by with the herd and had caught Sam's attention. He could not take his eyes off him. He did not use horses, but he knew when he saw fine horseflesh.

Knows Horses called Ollie, and he came forward. She rubbed her hands down his powerful legs and wiped the dust from his back. Sam walked closer, and Ollie appeared to not be alarmed by him. Sam was close and stretched out his hand so Ollie could smell it. Knows Horses watched closely. There was something good about this man. To be this close and Ollie's ears had not pricked forward and his nostrils had not flared.

Sam asked, "How many of his offspring looks like him?"

Knows Horses said, "Most do. Only a few have not shown his traits.

Any mares that cannot pass on his genes are removed from the brood stock."

The more he questioned her about the stallion, the more comfortable she became with him.

Sam looked at Knows Horses and said, "I believe you have found your gold in him. Have you sold any horses to any of the gold camps or sent them to San Francisco?" Sam was getting excited, thinking of the prices these horses would bring.

Knows Horses replied, "We have not. We want our valley to be a secret place."

Sam explained, "This place won't be a secret much longer. People are coming west in droves. There are men like me searching for gold in the mountains now. They will soon find this valley. They will kill for what is here." He pulled a stone from his pocket and showed it to her.

Knows Horses saw that it was gold and asked, "Where did you find this?"

Sam said, "When me and the burros stopped to drink at the stream. When the burros stepped out, the stone dislodged from the bank." Sam saw the dread in her eyes. "I checked the stream in other places and found nothing," he told her. "But I found a place that looked like it had been mined years ago."

Knows Horses knew what this man said was true. Their way of life was soon to be over. She could not let this man leave the valley alive. He would return with more men or speak of the gold to others.

She should have never let him live to see morning or become friendly with him. He had not threatened them in any way, as the others had done, but he did know what was here. Zack had said gold would drive white men crazy, like whiskey did the Indian.

Sam looked at her and knew that she was making a hard decision.

"I do not want your gold," he told her. "I am getting too old to enjoy spending it. I am only looking for a place to live out my life, hoping to find enough to keep me staked till I die."

Knows Horses had seen in this man something different, and so had Ollie.

"If I give you a job helping with the work around here, would you be willing to forget the gold?"

Sam said, "I really don't want the gold. I just love finding it. When I came to this valley, I knew it was here. Let me mine it for you when I am not working. It will be yours. All I ask is a place to stay and a stake to live on. Me and my burros don't need much."

Knows Horses explained the stories of the trappers that had come to take our gold. None had lived to carry it out of the valley. "I do not want to kill you," she said. "You seem to be a good man. I will give you a chance. If you lie, you will pay."

Sam gathered his burros and headed to the stream farthermost away. He would look there and then work his way back and report his findings. Sam had reached the spot he wanted so much to search. Ollie and the rest of the herd had also reached the area and were grazing peaceably. Sam set up camp and started panning and had found gold in no time.

He thought how, years ago, he would have been ready to kill for this claim. He thought about the women. They had been here all this time, knowing the gold was here but never touching it.

He looked around the flat grazing land, the beautiful mountains surrounding him as if he was in a bowl. Knows Horses and her family had found gold long ago and had chosen to not destroy this place. He would not either. He would obey the agreement he had made with Knows Horses. And what a fitting name, for she surely knew horses.

After a month of working the spot, Sam loaded up his find and carried it to Knows Horses. He had what he thought to be about fifty ounces.

Knows Horses realized that she had another problem now. She would have to get it to her hiding spot, without Sam seeing her. She hoped her husband and Warrior Woman would soon return.

CHAPTER TWENTY-SEVEN

It was another year before Zack and Warrior Woman returned to the valley they had missed so. Annie was set; she had made many friends. She had many young men wanting to come calling. She seemed to not be interested in any of them. She acted as if she knew that there was someone special for her and would not settle for less.

Knows Horses and Spring Flower were sitting on a bench under the shade tree when Ollie came by the cabin at a gallop and went out of sight. The women grabbed their guns and were getting prepared for unwanted visitors. Zack and Warrior Woman were coming down the trail in a wagon they had bought to make the trip. Knows Horses and Spring Flower ran to meet them.

Ollie had turned and was following the wagon. He must have smelled Zack or heard his voice. He was kicking his heels in the air like a young colt would have done. He was glad his old friend had returned.

As the family came together, Little Beth was not sure who these people were. She was being passed around, getting hugs and kisses. She was eager to be back on the ground.

Spring Flower and Knows Horses told Zack and Warrior Woman all that had happened since they had been gone. Zack seemed to be happy with the arrangement with Sam. The way Knows Horses had talked about him told him Sam would be an asset.

They had been to St. Louis and had seen the power of gold. They had studied themselves and had Annie learning about money. With what they had in the bank, plus the horses, cows, and the rest of the gold, they were rich in the white man's world.

Zack met Sam and enjoyed his company.

Sam said, "You have done right to keep the gold quiet and with protecting this place. When Knows Horses saw me at your cabin, I did not expect to live another day. If Ollie had not made me a friend, I am sure I would have been buried with one of her arrows in my back."

Zack told him, "We have fought many battles, and my wives do not hesitate to protect their family."

Sam sat down with us one night saying, "Civilization is coming, and you will need money. This valley that you have will need to be surveyed and titled. That will cost money. The government will take gold, but then people will know you have it. You have built a large herd of cattle and horses. Should you start selling them now, people would not suspect you have gold. You can sell your horses to the gold fields and silver mines."

We had never sold our horses before. We had only made trades with the Indians or given them as gifts to help someone who needed it.

Knows Horses agreed. She had come to trust this man she had almost put an arrow in the first day they met. She asked, "Will the miners want cattle too? How will we get them there?"

Zack said, "Black Elk and Many Kills might help us. I will ask if they might get some young warriors to go with us."

When Black Elk came, he brought three more warriors who had all benefited from their horses and an occasional beef.

They rounded up seventy steers and eight horses. Knows Horses would not be able to go with her beloved horses. Beth was too young to go and too young to leave behind. And she trusted Zack would not sell them to just anyone.

Zack asked Spring Flower to go with him on this trip, hoping to get her mind off Moon. Black Elk had brought news of their son. He was beginning to ride with warriors looking for trouble. They had already been in scrapes with other tribes.

Spring Flower said, "I will not leave in case he returns. Maybe I can speak to him and put him on the right path."

The cattle had proved to be a bigger job than expected. They were continually trying to go back home. The horses were tired and had to be changed out constantly. By the end of the first day, the cattle had worn themselves out and were ready to graze and lie down. Black Elk had located a camp with running water and plenty of grass for the animals.

Zack looked at Sam, complaining, "If I had known that getting cattle out of this valley would be so much trouble, I would never have brought them in."

Sam laughed and said, "They will settle down before long. They will get used to the trail."

The next morning, one of the first cows that had been brought in by Black Elk stood and walked to the front of the line. The rest followed. Zack had decided to sell her because of her age. He was fearful she would not last another year. The way she took charge and led the younger steers made Zack want to keep her. She could lead the herd in the future, but he knew that was not possible. She would not live to make a return trip.

At midday, Zack stopped the herd in a valley to drink and fill up on the grass that grew. It would not do to run all the fat off the cattle before reaching Silver City.

A few of the braves stayed with the herd just to keep them from spreading out too much. The rest stayed in camp and rested, waiting their turn to watch the cattle.

While Many Kills was watching the cattle, he spotted riders coming. He put his horse into a gallop, turning toward the camp. Waking the others, he let them know of the potential danger.

Five men who looked like trouble came riding into camp. They were the type of men who looked as if they had tried mining and decided it would be much easier to rob and steal than to work for what they got. What seemed to be the leader had a big grin on his face. He was looking over the Indian help we had.

The man introduced himself as Big Ben Brooks and said, "We have come to help you move these cattle. We heard that you might be having trouble, with the kind of help you have." He looked over at Black Elk with a sneer on his face.

"We are getting along just fine. We do not need or want any help. I would appreciate it if you would take your men and leave." I stood there, thinking I had made a mistake. We should have gotten to our weapons before these men came into our camp. But when I saw they were white men, I had told the camp we were in no danger. But Many Kills had been right.

Ben was looking at our weapons lying against the wagon. From the look on his face, he was fixing to make a move.

The other watchmen came riding from the herd and stopped behind the five men. Ben realized he should have made his move sooner; now it would not be as easy. He let out a big fake laugh and said, "We are going on back. We will watch the trail and make sure there are no rustlers ahead."

After they had left, we gathered everyone around, and I asked them their thoughts. Each man agreed we had not seen the last of Big Ben and his crew. Our herd was too big of a payday to let it get away. The horses along would be worth more than they had ever made.

Sam and I were trying to come up with some sort of strategy. Black Elk came up with the best idea.

He asked me, "Do we have to be in Silver City any particular time?"

I answered, "No rush. I am just wanting to be free of the worry. The cattle are eating and gaining weight."

Black Elk said, "We should let the cattle graze for a few days. We can set up watch, and if anyone chooses to return, we would be ready. When we do not move into the trap they have set for us, they will return. We will have a trap of our own. These sorts of men will not wait long. They know there is a lot of money to be made from your cattle. They will come soon."

We agreed, and Black Elk sent two warriors, Tracks Well and Two Toes, to follow the trail of Ben and his crew. They would know whether Ben had stopped to set a trap or left for good. The two warriors would see if Ben had more men waiting up the trail.

Ben and his men had been watching us from the beginning of our drive. They'd thought we would lose the herd when we were having so much trouble with them. When the old cow took the lead and the others fell in behind, we began to move. They had to come up with a new plan.

The next day, Tracks Well returned with news. Ben and his crew had set a trap, but there were only the five. One man had been sent from camp—whether to get more help or supplies, we didn't know. That left four. Two Toes had stayed to watch. After getting food and some supplies, Tracks Well headed back to keep watch.

I was lying in my blankets that night. After riding cattle, I was tired but could not go to sleep. I was not too worried about the rustlers. I felt we had a pretty good defense set up.

I thought about the time the first twin had come into our valley and his plans to take from us. I had allowed him to leave, only to find that Annie and Warrior Woman killed him that night. What would they have done about my present situation? They would have attacked. They would not be sitting around giving the rustlers time to build up their strength.

I got up and woke everyone. "We will attack the rustlers tonight. They are at their weakest; they are one man short. I do not want to wait until he returns with more men."

Black Elk and Many Kills were grinning from ear to ear; they were ready.

Sam and three braves were left to watch the cattle.

"If the rustlers come, do not fight. It is only cattle. We could take them back if we have to. But if my plan works, we will take care of them tonight."

Many Kills had gone before us to alert Tracks Well and Two Toes of our plan. They would meet us and lead us to Ben's camp.

When we meet the three, Many Kills said, "We will have to leave the horses and go in on foot." The rustlers had chosen their spot well. There was plenty of cover to fire on us from both sides, which they'd have done if we had tried to move the cattle through.

Our plan was for Many Kills and Tracks Well to move in on the south side and try to take one of the rustlers alive. Black Elk and Two Toes were to do the same on the north side. If we were successful, the two left would be easy.

The night was slipping by. None of the four warriors had returned, with or without a rustler. I was beginning to worry. They should have been back long ago. As the sky started to lighten in the east, I gathered the rest of my men, intent on going after them. As I was laying out my plan, Black Elk and the three warriors returned.

I asked Black Elk where the rustlers were. They had come back empty-handed.

"They are dead."

I was about to panic. I was not 100 percent sure that they were rustlers. Tracks Well and Two Toes, along with the other braves, did not understand my fear. I tried to make them understand. The white man's law was going to want me to show proof.

I had their bodies carried far away, hiding them as best we could.

We cleared their camp and brushed out any sign of tracks or fire pits. If we were lucky, we could run the cattle through their camp, and no trace of anything but cattle passing would be left.

I made the Indians release their horses and not keep any plunder from the rustlers that could be recognized later. We hurried back and got the cattle moving. We passed over the campsite, moving the cattle about ten miles before stopping for the night. We picked a place with good grazing and one that would be hard to attack without warning. Ben was the man who had left camp. I was sure he would come back.

All through the night, I tossed and turned, trying to decide. Should we turn back with the herd or go on? I knew from the experience with my wives that Indians dealt with problems far differently than did the white man. But times were changing.

Someone was going to ask questions about those men.

We were on the trail about two hours after the break of day when Big Ben and two more men rode up. It looked as if he thought his men had already taken the cattle and that he was coming to meet him. The smile on his face quickly disappeared when he saw me in the lead.

Ben roared, "Where are my men?"

"Right behind you."

Ben's blood looked as if it had all gone to his face. It was as red as an apple. "You know what I mean," he growled. "Where are the men I left to guard those cattle?"

The cattle had stopped, and my men began to gather round. This time, they were ready for trouble.

Ben was belligerent and said, "The sheriff will want to ask you some questions. I will see that you all hang."

"Ben, when you left my camp, you took your men. That was the last I saw of them. Why would you leave them to guard my cattle?"

Ben started to reply, but the bullet from Sam's gun tore him from his saddle. Before I could respond, the other two were on the ground.

I turned to Sam. When he saw my face, he knew what was coming. He shouted at me, cutting me off, "You have got to stop overthinking. If you have the drop on a thief and give him a chance, he will go away. But he will not leave you alone. These men would have killed us if we had not stopped them. Knows Horses told us before we left that you trust too easily and we would have to protect you."

Before I could give any orders, the men begin to clean up the mess, getting rid of the dead. We again ran the cattle over any sign we had made.

My Indian friends saw no wrong in what we had done. I could only hope we were at the end of our troubles.

As we got in sight of Silver City, three men came riding out to meet us. Just then, Sam quickly rode up beside me and said, "Black Elk is hurt and needs you to come to see about him."

I was worried about Black Elk, but I was more worried about the sheriff coming my way. Sam looked at me as if ordering me to go see about Black Elk.

The three men rode up to Sam. The first two introduced themselves as buyers for the cattle. The sheriff asked, "How did you manage to get through without rustlers taking your herd?"

Sam said, "We had no trouble. We have not met anyone since we left home."

The sheriff said, "Rustlers killed two other groups that tried to bring in beef. We figured out that it was Big Ben Brooks. We went out to arrest him. But he had changed his tactics and began taking cattle from the south. I had hoped that they had tried to take your herd and you had killed every one of the sons of bitches."

I meanwhile had arrived to check on Black Elk. He was making a fire and boiling coffee. He was supposed to be hurt. And where did he get coffee?

When I asked, he said, "From the first rustlers, and you should drink some."

"I need to get back and talk to the sheriff. I need to explain what happened."

Black Elk took a sip from his coffee, looked me in the eye, and said, "You are here, so there is no need to talk to the sheriff."

When Sam joined us, he apologized for tricking me. He and Black Elk explained to me that sometimes it was better to listen than talk. "The sheriff told me what you needed to know. These men were evil."

In Silver City, we were able to sell everything in two days and were promised that, if we could bring more, it would be bought.

I bought another wagon and a lot of supplies to take back. After returning from St. Louis, Warrior Woman had wanted to prepare some of the meals she had learned to cook but didn't have the right ingredients.

Along the way back, we ran into travelers headed to the mines. Most of the men seemed to be hardworking, just looking for a chance. Some looked as if they did not intend to do hard work. Usually, those were the ones that asked too many wrong questions. Some of them might wind up lost among the rocks, like Big Ben.

Black Elk and Many Kills were curious. "Where are all these men coming from?" Black Elk asked.

I explained that, when I went to St. Louis, even I was surprised about how much it had grown. I told them the white man would not stop. They had found riches and farmland. The Indians needed to learn to live a new life, or they would be rubbed out.

The rest of the trip was uneventful, and we were ready to get home.

We returned to the valley with the good news—we would be able to sell our stock for good prices.

Sam was proving his value more all the time. I told him, "I am glad Knows Horses did not kill you."

Zack I up an account at the bank that had been built in the town nearest our valley. There was record of our stock sales. With future sales, there should be no questions when we had to spend large amounts of money.

Sam had advised that, on each trip we made, we should take a bag of gold and deposit it. That should ensure that we would have the power to fight the white man's laws. We would be able to move the gold with the cattle, and no one would ever know.

CHAPTER TWENTY-EIGHT

In 1861, Annie returned, bringing with her a husband. His name was Hamil Davis.

War had broken out in the east, and Annie felt they should return to the safety of the valley.

Hamil was not the big, strong, outspoken man that had come calling when Zack and Warrior Woman were with her. He was the opposite. But he and Annie were always together and always happy, and the family seemed to find no wrong with him.

Hamil had studied to become a writer. He wrote novels and had wanted to come west to write about the American Indian.

When they were in St. Louis, Annie had used her allowance to support them. Hamil used his time to write. But when the war broke out, they'd decided that the valley would be the place to go. Now that he was here, he was able to work nonstop.

CHAPTER TWENTY-NINE

Over the years, the demand for horses and cattle was great. Knows Horses and I began looking for replacement bulls to upgrade our herds. We were always looking for a stallion to replace Ollie. He had grown old, and the past winter had been extremely hard on him. Knows Horses and I decided not to let him go through another hard winter. We agreed that, by the first snow, we would put him down.

It was late June, and Ollie had been unable to gain his weight back. It seemed that the joints in his legs were too sore to move. Most of the time, he stayed near the cabin.

Knows Horses went out early one morning to check on him. When she did not return for breakfast, I went out and found her lying across him, crying her heart out. He had died during the night. I only wished I would have been with him. I had been there when he had come into this world. I remembered how he had brought me to safety after I had been shot. I could only treat a friend like that with respect. I buried him close to Annie's grave. He had been part of my family from the start and our most loyal friend.

CHAPTER THIRTY

By the summer of 1865, it was time for Beth to go to school. Knows Horses had waited so long to have a child that turning lose was not easy. Annie had shared her experiences with her sister, but Beth was like Knows Horses. She loved the valley and did not want to leave it.

Knows Horses, Spring Flower, Beth, and I left for St. Louis. We had decided that, this time, we would buy a house. Spring Flower would stay with Beth until she had finished her schooling.

Knows Horses could not leave the horses long. If we left her in the city, she would be tempted to shoot most of the arrogant people.

We were able to find a house close to where we had boarded before. We walked the streets, letting the women get used to the ways of the modern world. Beth, like Annie, was a sensation from the start. People were looking at me and you could hear them whisper, "Squaw man."

After a month, Spring Flower and Beth seemed adjusted, and we felt it would be better for Knows Horses and me to leave. We did not want the attention toward me, with two wives, to leave a bad impression on Beth. Knows Horses had seen enough of the city. We said our good-byes and left. Knows Horses took it very hard, leaving her only child.

While we were in St. Louis, I had asked around the livery barns if there was anyone who had a good source of fine horses. I was told that a rancher in Independence had some fine breeding stock. On our way home, I wanted to take Knows Horses and try to find a new stallion.

We had arrived at the Circle C Ranch that was owned by Jack Carter.

While coming down the road, Knows Horses had gotten a look at some horses and seemed to be interested in the breeds. The handler came out to meet us, and you could tell he was not impressed with what he saw.

I told him, "I am looking to buy a stallion of good bloodlines."

The handler said, "You will not be able to afford any of our horses." He was looking at Knows Horses. In his eyes, I had become a squaw man and she, just an Indian squaw.

Holding my temper, I asked, "Can you show me some stallions that you have? I was told you have the best bloodlines around."

Instead, he had one of the workers bring out a horse that looked to be at least eight years old and was used to pull a wagon.

Knows Horses looked at him without moving and said, "We are not looking for a buggy horse."

The handler, acting rude, told us, "You cannot afford the worst horse that we have."

Lucky for him, the owner of the ranch came round the corral.

"Hello. My name is Jack Carter. Anything I can help you folks with?"

Knows Horses said, "We were told that you had a fine bloodline of stallions. Apparently, your handler does not know much about horses. We asked him to show us your best horse. This is what he thought your best looked like."

"I will deal with our guest," Mr. Carter told his handler. "Take that nag out of here and get to work, doing what I apparently overpay you for."

Mr. Carter liked Knows Horses from the start. He took us in the stables to show us the horses he was training for market. He began to explain to us the bloodlines.

We came to a stall that had a long-bodied horse. He had well-muscled shoulders and hips, with a small head. He explained that the horse had Arabian blood; he had great speed and endurance.

Knows Horses asked, "Can you bring this stallion out in the light? I would like to look closely at him."

Jack Carter told us, "I have just started training this horse. He is green broke."

Knows Horses, speaking in her native language, walked to the stallion. She was looking at him and checking all of his muscles.

The stallion was smelling Knows Horses. He seemed to be listening to every word she spoke.

Mr. Carter repeated himself, "He is only green broke. Don't let her to close."

Knows Horses jumped on the stallion's back, wheeled him around, and set out down the road. She gave the horse rein and let him run.

The ranch hand who had brought the stallion out for Knows Horses said, "I will get my horse and see if I can catch her before she gets hurt or, worse, hurts the stallion."

Laughing, Mr. Carter said, "I don't think you will catch her. She will return when she is ready." Mr. Carter dismissed him. He turned to me. "Do you want to come in for coffee while we wait on Knows Horses?"

As we drank our coffee, I explained our line of breed and our need for a new stallion. "Knows Horses has developed our own bloodline. That is where her name comes from."

Mr. Carter showed me books that he had from all over the world on horses. The pages featured photos, along with descriptions of many breeds. I thought that Ollie should have been in this book. They were his equals, but none was better.

We heard the thunder of rider and horse returning and went out to meet her. When she got off she said, "I will take him."

Mr. Carter said, "Maybe, but you don't even know his price."

Knows Horses said, "I give you one thousand dollars."

"You have just bought yourself a fine horse. Why would you offer so much without asking what I wanted for him?"

Knows Horses said, "That is his value, and I will not haggle. I do not wish him to think he is worth less."

We were invited to spend the night. Mr. Carter and his wife treated us very well, asking us the next morning to stay longer. They had so many questions about our breed of horses and the valley where we lived. We promised to stop by the next time we came through and visit longer.

On our way home, most of the time, Knows Horses was riding the stallion. I brought the wagon. She would ride in great circles around the wagon, making sure that no danger was coming our way. She and the horse were beautiful. They moved as one. Taking long strides, the horse acted as if he wanted her on his back.

"What made you pick that particular horse?"

"Did you not here him speaking to me? He told me his breed had come from the desert—that he can endure without water longer than other breeds. When we mix him with Ollie's bloodline, our horses will be even stronger."

We came into our valley, and it looked as it did the very first time I had seen it. We had been careful not to kill all the beaver. They still maintained the ponds that were essential to the valley.

The surrounding mountains with snow on the tops reminded me of that day long ago when Ollie and I first saw them. We'd come to the spot where I'd left my packs and found my wives. I did not ever want to leave our valley again.

Knows Horses named the stallion Rocky, after I had said he belonged in the Rockies. Now he was smelling the mares and wanting to go to them. She released him, and what a beautiful sight he was going across the valley.

As I watched him run, my mind was on Ollie. He had stolen the mares from another stallion and had sired plenty of his own.

As I watched, I told Knows Horses, "He will only take over the job Ollie started. He will never replace him."

Hamil was always writing, taking notes—that is, when he and Annie were not riding over the valley. It reminded me of the times my wives and I had done the same years earlier. It seemed like they were reliving our lives. They would always have camping gear and sometimes stayed out for days.

When Hamil was around us, he was always interested in the history we had shared. He was continually asking questions about our past.

Warrior Woman was happy they had decided to come back to our valley and was always hoping for a grandchild. She talked of this with me. I told her that, when the time was right, it would happen.

CHAPTER THIRTY-ONE

The year was 1870. I was somewhere around sixty years old.

Beth had returned. She was a beautiful, refined young woman. When she returned, a young lady named Donna Dixon came home with her.

Donna was headed to San Francisco to work in the newspaper business. She said that she and her brother had a little inheritance. With it, she was going to set up a printing press. As soon as her brother was able to complete all of their business transactions, he would bring the money and would meet her there. He was to join her in San Francisco. He would stay with her till her printing business was up and running.

Donna could not say enough about her brother. He always had her best interest at heart. He had tried to give her all of their money—then she would not have to work—telling her he could make his way in life.

Hamil, being an author, questioned her about her printing press. She was hesitant to say much and stayed away from that conversation. It seemed to be something she knew very little about. Yet she was planning to invest a lot of money into it. Maybe her brother was the one who would run the press.

That summer, we were getting cattle and horses ready to sale. Hamil had finished another novel and would go with the herd to send his book to his publisher.

Donna had decided it was time to return to St. Louis. She would join her brother and travel with him to San Francisco.

As she was saying good-bye, she promised, "I will stop on my way to San Francisco to visit with you again."

Beth nodded, with tears in her eyes. She would miss her friend, who she felt was more like a sister.

Donna was on the stage headed back to St. Louis. Hamil had sent his novel with her to give to his publisher. The cattle and horse sales had been deposited. We had ordered new furniture for the cabin and a hay mower the year before. With our wagons loaded, we headed home.

Sam rode along beside me, and we talked of the things that we had accomplished.

"Sam, I want you to take some money and enjoy your life while you can."

He just smiled. "Where would I go? What can money buy that I don't already have? I can't think of a thing I would enjoy more than being with family."

Sam had become as much a part of our family as anyone could. He continually worried about the future—what we must do to protect our valley and our children's rights to it.

In late fall, Donna returned with her brother, Kyle. He was a handsome young man a few years older than Donna. As soon as he stepped to the ground, he headed to Beth and took her hand. He began with how much he had heard about her from Donna and looked forward to getting to know her. As their visit lengthened, he started to follow Beth around, monopolizing much of her time.

Knows Horses was thinking about putting an arrow in his belly. He had brought no presents, as was the custom. When he would place his hand on her daughter, Knows Horses knew, it did not sit well with Beth. He seemed to think that his good looks and smooth talk were all he needed to get what he wanted in this world. He still had a lot of learning to do.

Donna and Kyle seemed to be in no hurry to leave. Kyle was following Beth so closely that, if she stopped, he would run into her. He was proving to be a nuisance. When he was asked to help with the cattle or gather wood, he would always say that Beth had plans for him, or he was inviting her on a picnic.

Beth asked me, "What do you feel about Kyle?"

"I do not know what a woman looks for in a man," I told her. "If he were what you wanted, I would not interfere. I have noticed that he is a mite lazy. But back in St. Louis most of the people did not seem to do much. He may have had enough money that he has had servants to do the manual labor. If you chose him and stay in the valley, he will have to learn our ways and work hard as everyone else does."

As the warm fall days drifted by, Beth tried to spend as much time with the horses and her mother as she could. This irritated Kyle, because Knows Horses did not allow him near her horses.

Trying to get his way, Kyle would ask Beth to take him places in the valley or on picnics. When the two of them were alone, he was always trying to push himself on her.

It was at the point that she decided to speak to Knows Horses. She was a little afraid to bring the issue up with her mother, as Kyle was her friend's brother. As hosts, she and her family were expected to entertain their guests. Over the years, she had heard how the women in her house handled bad situations. She would hate to have to tell her friend that her brother was dead because of her mother.

We had been thinking, or hoping really, that our guests would be leaving soon. They had stayed on even though we had explained that the passes would soon be covered with snow. Now it was too late for them to leave. The passes were closed, and it would be spring before they melted.

Beth worried about being shut up all winter with Kyle; she feared that she would not be able to tolerate him or able to keep Knows Horses from killing him. Knows Horses was tolerating him now. But Beth could see that it would not last much longer.

Spring Flower came up with the solution. Knows Horses and Warrior Woman took Kyle and Donna to Spring Flower's cabin. Knows Horses told them, "You can stay here during the winter. We feel you will enjoy the cabin and having time to yourselves. We will see that you have all the things you will need. You may visit us if you need anything. Zack will bring you a side of beef; we will also bring wild meat throughout the winter."

Warrior Woman said, "There is some wood in the sheds, but you will need to gather more. What is there will not be enough."

Somehow Donna and Kyle had not seen this coming. They would have to wait on themselves.

Kyle could not understand why Beth did not come and stay with him through the winter. It was bad enough that he was having to eat wilderness food. Now he was expected to cook it himself. In St. Louis, there were many young girls who would jump at the chance to share his bed and make him as comfortable as possible. These backwoods people would treat him differently after he married Beth and gained control of their wealth. They apparently did not know how to enjoy life.

He would give Beth a couple weeks without him. He would go visit her. He knew she would be glad to come back with him then.

He was even having trouble with Donna. Did she expect him to stay in that cabin all winter without sex? The few times that he had been able to get her in his bed, it was as if she was doing him a favor.

CHAPTER THIRTY-TWO

The first snow had come, and it was deep. It was the worst snow this early that they could remember. Hamil had been caught out in it; he'd been returning from a trip to Sam's camp. Sam had become a colorful character and was providing him with good material. In the beginning, he had caught a bad cold and had stayed in the cabin working on his next book. But sick or not, being closed up in the cabin did not suit him. He'd wanted to make another visit to Sam's camp. He had not realized how cold it really was. He was close to freezing on his return home. That night, he began to cough. For weeks after, he had no strength and could not get well. It seemed to be gradually getting worst. Annie had been doing all the chores and tending to Hamil. She asked Beth to come and help her. While she was looking after Hamil, and tending her house, she was getting no sleep and had begun to cough herself.

Zack went to Spring Flower's cabin to check on their guest. He advised Kyle and Donna to stay close to the cabin and inside all they could. As he was leaving, he told them he had to go to Annie's. Hamil and Annie were sick, and Beth had gone there to help them.

Donna had all the news she needed. She immediately moved, uninvited, to help Beth with the sick—which meant Beth had another person to look after.

But Donna was a surprise; she actually worked, helping with cleaning the house or sitting with Hamil. In the days that followed, she and Beth fell into a schedule. She would read Hamil's novels to him so he could make corrections. She had arranged to become the night nurse. She would sit with the sick at night and let Beth sleep. She did all that was asked of her.

She did not want to go back to the cabin with Kyle. He continually wanted her in bed to pass the boring hours away. So far, she had not become pregnant. But it would only be a matter of time. She was too close to her goal. She did not want to explain a child between what was believed to be brother and sister.

Kyle felt he had been abandoned. He knew Beth was with Annie, but so was Donna. Surely Donna would give Beth time to come to come visit him and share his bed. He, a respectable man, who had lain with the beauties of St. Louis, was banished to this dingy cabin. And to be expected to wait on himself? *When I marry this little Indian*, he told himself, *she will pay for the way she has abandoned me.* He became furious when he thought about her staying with a sick man, tending to his needs, instead of being with him—her future husband.

When he was in charge of her and her wealth, she would learn what it was like to be abandoned through the long, cold winter months. He would find a way to leave and enjoy the San Francisco life. He knew that she would not be able to resist him much longer. All he had to do was remain patient, and after a while, she would not be able to resist any longer. She had been more of a challenge than the women in St. Louis. Even the older women who thought they could resist his charms sooner or later gave in and opened their purses.

Donna had found Hamil's autobiography of the Morris family. Over the years, he had gathered information on Annie's family. He was so interested in their history that he had to put it on paper—Zack and Ollie, Spring Flower, the whole family. He was fascinated with what they had gone through. And in the end, it had all worked out for them. Hamil had written of the gifts that Zack had given, not knowing that in the native culture that was how you bought a wife, or wives on some occasions. He'd written of the gold and the thieves who had thought it would be easy to come and take what they wanted.

He knew he would never be able to publish it. This family had never been concerned with riches outside their valley. He had come to love it and did not want to change it in any way. He also knew that it was history. Their story needed to be written for the generations that would follow.

Donna reread the part where they had found the gold and decided not to use it for wealth. She knew that Knows Horses had hidden the gold. She believed the only one who would know where it was buried would be Beth. Zack and his wives had used some but had left most for their children. It would be for them to use in the future. She knew they had spent very little. Maybe they had used some for the girls' schooling?

CHAPTER THIRTY-THREE

Donna had met Beth in school and noticed how all the young boys followed her around, conveniently showing up wherever she went. Donna became her friend, staying close by her side.

On a shopping trip together, Beth had to run by the bank before it closed to get some money. The older bank teller seemed to fall all over himself trying to accommodate her. He was close to forty but seemed to have an eye for the younger women. Donna had taken notice of how he had looked at their bodies. She might be able to get some information from him, if she played him right.

The following Saturday night, they had been invited to a party. A carriage had been sent to pick Beth up. Donna had made arrangements to be there to ride with her. She wanted to step out of the same carriage that Beth arrived in. Maybe by doing so, she could attract some young man that would send a carriage for her.

While at the party, all the wealthy young men danced with and surrounded Beth. They were plenty of young men talking and dancing with Donna, but none of them were rich enough for her liking. She could get all the poor boys she wanted. But being poor and tending to a bunch of kids was not what she wanted out of life.

The following week, Donna went to Beth's bank. She waited for the teller who had handled Beth's transaction. "William Peterson, Assistant Manager," was written on his office door.

As he ushered her into his office, Donna stopped fast, making him bump into her. When he grabbed her to keep her from falling, he held her a little too long. He led her to a chair, apologizing and offering to get her some coffee or water.

Donna pretended she would like to set up an account like Beth's. She told him that, since Beth used him, she felt she could trust him. She said that he seemed more mature than the person she had been using.

William Peterson was looking as she crossed her legs, causing the split in her skirt to fall open, leaving her leg exposed. He tried to seem as though he was not staring and was tending to the business at hand. He had never been able to even see Beth's ankle.

He begin asking, "How much money would you like to deposit? I will need to know the expenses that you pay. This way, I can set you up a budget. I will invest your money, so it will not run out." •

Donna said, "I only have a few minutes. I wanted to meet you personally. Would it be possible for you to meet me tomorrow—maybe at the restaurant at my hotel—to talk more? This is such a big step for me, and I do not wish to be rushed."

William Peterson agreed. "Yes it is a big step, but there is no way I will allow anyone to take advantage of you."

He walked her to the door and assured her that he would be there at six o'clock tomorrow. As he walked back to his office, he was wondering what excuse he could use to get away from his wife. Something told him he needed to keep this young lady a secret.

Donna went to the Charles House off the main drag. To make her plan work, she had to make him feel comfortable. By coming to this lesser known hotel, he would be unlikely to run into his more important clients. She had made arrangement for a room the following evening.

Donna asked Beth a lot of questions about budgets and how much was a fair amount to deposit. She told Beth she was afraid to put all her money in one place, as she could not afford to lose any.

Beth said, "I don't know much about banks. My parents made a deposit large enough to get me by until I go home. I have no idea how much. My banker says I always underspend. He says with the interest the money is making, he could allow me to spend more than I was originally given when he made my budget."

The following day, Beth had promised Spring Flower that they would go shopping. Following that, they would go to a nice restaurant for dinner.

They had been gone from the mountains for a long time and were homesick for their valley and the beautiful scenery there. In the city, all you saw was buildings and people, so many people. They felt that the city was filthy and could not understand why so many would want to stay in the same filthy place all the time. They would be glad the day school was out and they would be able to start home.

Spring Flower asked Beth, "What do you plan to tell all your young men when school is over and we go home?"

Beth said, "I have not led them to think that I would be staying in the city. They are only friends. I have never promised them anything."

That evening, Donna had checked in early. For her plan to work, she needed to be as attractive as she could.

William Peterson arrived early to get a seat where they would not be in full view of the sidewalk traffic. He was nervous, but he felt that, if he was a gentleman, she would feel more comfortable around him. The young lady was beautiful. Why had she invited him to meet with her outside the office, unless she really was interested in him? Maybe one day, he might get invited to her room.

When Donna was shown to his table, they ordered. He had ordered her wine and began to question her as to the account that they would be setting up.

She wanted to talk more about his role in the bank and wanted to wait until they had their meal before they talked business.

As the evening went along, his role at the bank began to grow. He was soon telling her all of his secrets for running the bank. The doors would close without him. She knew that he was trying to impress her with his knowledge of money.

They had their meal and drank more wine. When she felt the time was right she said, "I really do not feel right talking business at the table. There are so many people around. I do not want anyone to overhear my business. Would you mind if we went to my room? I would feel more comfortable there."

William Peterson replied, "I will do whatever puts you at ease. I know answering all my questions will be personal. I can understand you wanting to answer them in private." He could not believe his luck. This was moving much faster than he had hoped.

When they reached her room, she handed him the key.

William had trouble opening the lock. She could see his hands shaking. He got the door unlocked, they entered, and Donna went to the small table and put her purse down. She turned to him, walking slowly. If she played him right, he would never know that he was giving her information about Beth.

William watched this beautiful young woman walk to him slowly; as she came, she was disrobing. He could not believe his eyes; his heart was beating so rapidly he thought that it would burst. When she was at arm's length, he pulled her close, kissing her. She returned the kiss.

"I hope you do not think of me as being a lose woman. From the first time I met you, I have not been able to get you off my mind. It is so unfair that Beth does not appreciate you."

William finished undressing her and then pulled his clothing off. He was picking her up and laying her on the bed, and she was pulling him to her.

After sex, when William was able to untangle from her, he realized that it was going to be hard to leave this beautiful woman. What was it she had said? That Beth did not appreciate him? He needed to find out if Beth planned to move her account. As large as it had grown, the bank would miss investing it.

"What did you mean when you said your friend, Beth, did not appreciate me? Is she displeased with the bank?"

"Oh she is a little spoiled girl. You work for her, but she does not appreciate what you do. Other people have to support her. She depends on her poor family to pay her way. I have to make it on my own."

"Beth's family is not as poor as you might think," he told her. "They brought enough gold to support her for years. They did the same for her older sister. But when you look at them, you would think they have nothing."

She said, "Let's not talk about Beth. Come. Be with me. I will not see you again for a while."

"Are you going away?"

"No, but you are a married man. We cannot make this a habit. We might get caught. Such a fine man like you does not need his life destroyed by a young girl. I know I can only see you now and then. In a month or two, I will get in touch with you again."

William, after making love again, was satisfied that he could wait a month for this prize. He began to think, *Once a month—who would ever know?* He would be set up.

Donna had the information she needed. Her plan was beginning to move forward. Now she had to avoid William. Maybe he would not ask Beth about her.

Donna had come up with a plan. She would travel home with Beth, if she could find a way to get invited. Beth's home had been a topic that they did not talk about much. It had caused Donna's imagination to run wild.

Donna decided that Beth's family must have a large gold mine and was trying to keep its location a secret. She had heard of people who were rich and acted as if they had nothing. She knew that, if she was able to get her hands on that gold, she would live in a fine home and have servants wait on her.

Donna had another piece of the plan that had to be ironed out before school was over. Beth would leave the day after school closed. She talked of nothing else.

Donna had a friend who she felt would go along with her plan—for a share of the goods. Kyle Burk was known for playing around with the affections of women in order to get what he wanted in life. She arranged to meet him one day before school was over. She pointed Beth out and asked, "Would you be willing to marry her for a small fortune?"

Kyle looked at what he thought was the most beautiful woman in St. Louis. He knew this was going to be one of the best and most rewarding games he had ever played. Kyle told Donna, "Introduce me now before she leaves. She may have a young friend back home. I will have a better chance to get her now."

Donna said, "That is not the way this is going to work. We have to gain her confidence. You must never act as though you know she has money. I am planning to travel to her home, and later, after I have gained her family's trust, I will come for you."

Lately, Donna had decided that Kyle had become a problem. He had pushed to hard in the beginning. He thought his good looks would open all doors. They did with the bored city women. Maybe she should have explained that all the young men in St. Louis had tried to impress Beth. She seemed to not even notice them. She would go to their parties and go out with a crowd. But she was never alone with any of them.

Now, somehow, she needed to get Kyle out of the valley. The only way this plan would work now would be for him to leave. If Beth missed him enough, he could be brought back later—as long as he was gone before there was a scandal.

Donna knew that Hamil was not getting better. If he should pass, she would be sent back to stay with Kyle. There, she knew that he would force her to have sex with him, risking a baby. She had to start developing a plan to get him out of the valley—at least for now.

When there was a break in the weather and it had warmed a bit, Zack announced he would go to see about Kyle. Donna went along, under the pretense that she needed to make sure that Kyle was doing all right. She told Zack she could not risk her brother getting sick. He was the only kin she had. If anything happened to him, she would be alone in this world.

When they arrived at the cabin, it was clear Kyle was a little upset. But Zack seemed not to notice. Kyle put on a show. He told Donna, "I am glad that you have helped Annie. I know how hard it is to get through these trying times."

Donna said, "Right now, I am concerned with your health. I will stay with you and cook you a good meal. Beth is with Annie, and I can return later."

After Zack left, Kyle started his threats. "I will expose everything if there's not some changes soon. I did not agree to be shut up in a cabin by myself all winter long. Hell, I thought I would have Beth with me. But I wound up with you, and then you were gone."

It was kind of funny to her, but she could not let him see her laugh. She would have to risk getting pregnant again. She needed to calm him down. He had to understand that he would have to leave—the sooner the better for her. She had to find a way to get him out safely.

Kyle settled down. He was happy to be leaving as soon as it could be arranged. After Donna left to go back to Annie's, he began to form his own plan.

Before Donna returned to Annie's. She had a talk with Knows Horses and the rest of the family. She asked, "Would there be any way for Kyle to go on to San Francisco? We were supposed to meet the ships bringing my printing press. I am afraid that it will be shipped back if we do not make arrangements to store it. I have been so busy helping Annie with Hamil that I forgot about the press.

"Kyle is very worried about missing the ship. He is thinking of trying to make the trip alone. I do not want him to, but we seem to have no choice. We have most of our money tied up already. If we lost it, we would never be able to regain our loss."

After Donna left, we began to try to find a way for Kyle to leave. He had been a problem ever since he had arrived.

Knows Horses had an idea, but it involved killing him. The family got a good laugh, but I think she was serious.

The weather had continued to warm. Sam and I felt that we could make it. We might have to use snowshoes in some spots, but it was possible, as long as we did not get another blizzard. It was set. We would give it one more week, and if the weather did not get any worse, we would be on our way.

Donna informed Kyle that he would be leaving and advised him to be ready. She told him, "Mind your manners and wait in Silver City. I will find an excuse to go with the cattle drive this summer. I will bring you word. Beth is beginning to worry a little. If you remain quiet, we can still get the gold. And it is much more than I had thought."

Anything she could think of to get him gone and keep his mouth shut, she would tell him. She did not dare tell him that she felt that the whole family was happy to see him go. She would breathe a sigh of relief to see him gone.

Kyle could not help but think that Beth being away from him had produced the effect that he knew it would. Women could not resist him. This one had been different and more difficult than normal. But staying away from her was having the effect he wanted.

CHAPTER THIRTY-FOUR

Zack, Sam, and Kyle were mounted and going through the pass. They hated leaving fresh tracks that could lead warring Indians a trail into their valley. But it was still a little early, and maybe they were staying close to their teepees.

They were headed west, and Kyle seemed to be sticking with the plan. He was happy to have someone to talk with, even if he had to share the work when they made camp. He tried to seem concerned and worried that they may have lost Donna's inheritance.

When we reached the high pass, the horses did their best but were not able to get through the deep snow. We stopped and unloaded everything and let the horses return.

Kyle watched as the horses were set free. He knew that he would have to walk. There were packs that would have to be carried on their backs.

We put on our snowshoes and took what we could of our supplies and headed over the pass. It was hard going with the snowshoes and packs on our backs. We would stop and rest, but we had to keep moving. We could not risk getting trapped if another storm came. By pushing on, only stopping for brief rests, we made good time. After two days, we were able to leave off the snowshoes and move at a better pace, stopping and resting along the way.

We were about two days from Silver City when we met a young man about twenty-two years of age. He looked as if he had not eaten in a week. We made camp and fixed him a meal and asked about his current situation.

"My name is Benjamin Pruitt. I came looking for my fortune with a friend. We hit a fairly good strike. Somebody was watching, and we got jumped. My friend was killed, and everything we had was lost. After everything I've been through, I'm giving up. I was lucky to get out with my life."

Sam said, "If you continue on in that direction, you won't have a life for long. You will need better clothing and plenty of food, and you have neither. It would be better to travel with us. We can spare you food; you can help carry our packs for trade."

Ben knew that the men were right and that he had run into the first luck on this entire trip. He hooked up with the three and did twice the work around camp. He carried extra weight to help the older men. Ben proved to be a friendly young man, with a much better attitude than Kyle's. He and Sam got along great, talking about mining and horses.

Ben asked, "Why did you attempt this trip without horses?"

I explained, "We started with horses, but we turned them lose so they could return home. They would not have made it through the snow."

Ben said, "I bought a big buckskin horse two years ago. That horse had more stamina than any I have ever owned. Now, the claim jumpers have him."

Sam told Ben, "We are going to deliver Kyle and then get back to home as soon as possible. We have no interest in trying to recover your losses. Doing so may get someone hurt or killed."

I watched Ben. He knew how to work. He did not wait to be told what to do. If he saw a thing needed doing, he would get up and get it done.

"Ben, would you consider working for me? Sam and I are getting a little too old to keep up with the cattle and horses. These trips are getting longer every year, and it won't be long before we can't make the drive."

Ben knew he had no other option, and he liked his present company. He agreed to give it a try.

Kyle had heard the conversation and felt that he needed no competition with Beth. He had frozen his butt off in that damn cabin, and he intended to collect his prize. When he had the chance, he would talk with Ben.

As soon as he'd gotten Ben away from Sam and Zack, Kyle told him, "You will be better off going back where you come from. The winters are rough, and the work is hard. I have been here almost a year. The only reason I am going to return is to marry my bride, Beth. She is Zack's daughter. She is waiting for my return." Kyle tried to get it through Ben's head that Beth was his.

"I can't see what any of that has to do with me working at the ranch," Ben told him. "I'm needing a place to work, not looking for a wife."

Ben had been raised doing this work his whole life. Now he saw a chance to get paid for the things that he was already doing. He thought Kyle was a spoiled city dude, used to getting his way. He hoped that, when they got to Zack's ranch, Kyle would hurry and marry his Beth and be on his way. Something about him just didn't sit well with Ben.

When we reached Silver City, I went to the bank. Sam and I had brought a bag of gold apiece. I needed to get them to the bank without anyone knowing about it. I needed to talk with the bank manager.

The bank manager was busy when I walked in. He looked up and saw me waiting. When he'd finished with his costumer, he came by my side.

"Mr. Morris, how nice to see you. What can I do for you today? Bringing more gold, I hope." He smiled. "Come into my office; less people to hear your business."

When the door closed, I said, "I have more gold, and I want to discuss some upcoming changes. I want Beth to start handling the account. I need to make sure there will be no problems if something happens to me."

Meanwhile, Sam had gone to the hotel with Kyle. Once he'd gotten him settled in, the two said their good-byes.

"It feels like a breath of fresh air getting rid of that idiot," Sam said once we'd met back up. "His sister seems to be taking care of him, instead of him taking care of her."

We went to the livery barn to purchase horses for the return trip. Ben appeared to have a good eye for horses. And none shied away from him as he touched them. His hands had a gentle touch.

I believed that, with the snow still melting, the horses would have a better chance of getting through. I bought a small sled to haul our supplies. When we got back to the deep snow, we could put snowshoes on and walk. The horses should be able to get through carrying less weight.

We stopped at the store to buy supplies. While there, we decided to buy some of the new repeating rifles and pistols that had been developed. I thought that, if we'd had those guns when the Indians had attacked, Annie would still be alive.

As I thought of Annie, I went to the stone carver and put in an order for two headstones—one for Annie and one for Ollie. I would pick them up when we returned in the summer. I felt they needed to always be remembered.

The trip home proved harder than we'd expected. When we finally got through the pass, the horses were worn out. We stopped for a day to let them rest. We still had a long way to go. The horses needed their strength if they were going to make it home.

Sam spoke to Ben of the valley. The closer we got, the more excited Ben seemed to get. He had a job, with a cabin to live in, and he'd actually be getting paid. He would be working with men he liked and respected. Maybe his luck had changed.

As we turned into the pass, Ben wondered aloud how we had ever found it. He had not seen it until we were entering. We told him of Two Mountains and the trades we had made—how we'd essentially traded the use of the packhorses for this valley.

On the other side of the pass, Ben could not believe the view before him. It was too beautiful to describe—streams running down the canyon, beaver ponds that had been built over the years, spruce trees, and signs of wildlife everywhere. And somewhere in there was a herd of cattle and horses.

They took him to Spring Flower's cabin, where Kyle had stayed. He could take his time and get settled in. He could rest a day or so. Then he could come down to the big cabin and meet the rest of the family.

CHAPTER THIRTY-FIVE

Ben found the cabin in a complete mess. Whoever had previously stayed there had not bothered to clean. There were bones and dirty dishes. The bed clothing had not been cleaned.

That would be the first on his list—washing the bed clothing and hanging it out to dry. His skin crawled, thinking of sleeping in such a mess. He felt that it would make a fine home, but he would not live in those conditions. With a little elbow grease, he could fix it up just fine.

Donna heard a conversation about a new hand living in the cabin. She needed to check out who Zack and Sam had brought in the valley. She realized from what had been said that whoever the new addition was, he was young and a hard worker. She did not need him interfering in her plans.

"I feel I need to go help the new hand clean the cabin. I fear that Kyle has left it in a mess. He has never been one to be concerned with such things," she told Warrior Woman. "And this Ben may not know how to clean himself."

When she was in sight of the cabin, she watched from cover. She needed to learn as much about him as she could before she approached.

Ben washed the clothes at the pool and was hanging them on a rope that he had stretched between two trees. This was the last of it; he had washed and hung out everything he could find. Now he was going to clean the filthy pans that were piled inside.

This man was completely different from Kyle. He was not as good looking. He seemed to be a working man and one who liked a clean home. When she thought of lying in those dirty bedclothes with Kyle, it made her shiver. She decided that Beth might be interested in this kind of man. The charm and good looks of Kyle had not impressed her.

Donna, moving her horse into view, called, "Hello. Is it all right to stop and visit?"

Ben was excited; here in the wilderness was a young girl about his age. She appeared to be friendly. Then he thought, *Oh maybe this is Kyle's "Beth." Oh well,* he reasoned, *I can at least be nice. This is Zack's daughter.*

"Won't you come in? I just cleaned the coffeepot and have just put some on. Would you like a cup?" He thought, *If she is Beth, I can see why Kyle was so smitten.* She was very attractive. *And spoken for,* he reminded himself.

"You must be Beth. I'm Ben. I met your future husband on the trail."

"No, no. I am not Beth. I am Donna, and Kyle is my brother. But I would love a cup of coffee." Donna entered the cabin, noticing that it was as clean as when she and Kyle had moved in. Ben still had dishes to wash, but her cup had been cleaned. He had been very busy.

Over coffee, Donna began asking questions. She found Ben to be very pleasant. She thought that, if she could hook him before he saw Beth, she might be able to keep him from being a future problem. Besides, she would not really mind going to a clean bed with him. This might even give her more reasons to stay or return if she had to leave for some reason.

Donna finished her coffee, got up, and started scrubbing the dirty dishes.

Ben jumped up, saying, "I will do that. I have not been here long. I do not live in filth. This mess was left by someone else. I was going for the dishes when you came. You don't have to help."

"But I do," Donna said. "It was my brother who left this mess. I planned to come up here in another day or two to clean it. I am sorry. He is not used to living alone. But that is no excuse, really." She looked around. "I will do these dishes. You can stack more wood for the fire. Nights are cold here." She needed to stay a while. She knew she could get him interested in her if she had a little time.

After the dishes were done and the firewood had been stacked, Ben told Donna, "Since you are here, we can ride together to Zack's. I am ready to meet the rest of the family."

Donna almost panicked. She knew that, when he saw Beth, he would fall head over heels in love with her. She would miss her chance, and her plans could go astray. She acted as if her feelings had been hurt.

Ben moved close to her and asked, "Are you all right? Have I said something wrong? I did not mean to."

Donna said, "I know we have only known each other for a few hours. I feel like you are someone I would like to be friends with. I thought, after you had been on the trail a long time, you would like a good meal. I can cook for you, and we could get to know each other better. I feel like it would be a good thing to do, but if you want me to leave, I will."

Not wanting to hurt anyone, Ben said, "I have been on the trail too long. I cannot tell you the last good cooked meal I had. I would love for you to stay and cook. I am in no hurry for you to leave."

Donna took her time cooking the meal. It was almost dark when they began to eat. After the meal, she brought Ben a cup of coffee and then started washing up the dishes.

While she worked, she talked of Zack and his wives. Finishing the dishes, she sat down and told the story of how Annie had let her long hair down and allowed Zack to see how beautiful she was.

She let her hair fall to show Ben how Annie had done it. Then she said that Annie had walked over and let her clothes fall, showing Zack her beautiful body. Donna stood, dropped her clothing, and turned around to see the affect it had on Ben.

He picked her up and gently laid her in his bed. They made love long into the night. When morning came, Ben tried to remember just how all this had come about. Donna stirred, pulled him to her, and they made love again.

Donna felt Ben was under her control. He would remember the night he'd had with her. When he met Beth, and she showed him no attention, as she had the young men at school, he would naturally come to her.

She left him early. She wanted to spread the news of what a good friend she had made. Maybe Beth would see that Ben cared about her. Beth, being her friend, would keep him at a distance. It was unfair. Beth could have any man she wanted, and she had all the gold she could ever spend.

Ben, waking, found Donna gone. He lay in bed, amazed at how his life had turned around. A month ago, he'd had the hell beaten out of him and lost his best friend. He'd had his claim taken from him—a claim they had worked hard to get producing. He had been almost starved when Zack and Sam had saved his life.

Now I have a job and home, Ben thought. And last night? What was he to make of that? Meeting Donna and what had followed had been totally unexpected. Now I had to keep it, best quit dallying and get to it.

When Ben came out of the timber and saw the open valley with deep grass, he could not comprehend the vastness of it. There were cattle scattered over the southern end and horses on the northern end. A person who had never seen it could never dream of anything this beautiful.

Right in the middle was a large cabin. You did not see cabins this big or nice. Most were just something thrown up to get by. Who were these people?

As Ben arrived at the cabin, everyone came out to meet him, or so he thought. A young girl walked out, one that all women wanted to look like. She had a beautiful smile and was very friendly. This young woman did not seem to know how beautiful she was. She was barefoot, and she did not seemed concerned that she was a bit dusty and dirty.

Knows Horses stepped up, saying, "Beth, this is Ben. We have talked of him working with the horses. We will have to see what the horses think."

Donna quickly saw his reaction and came to his side. She introduced him, making sure everyone knew that she had staked her claim.

Acting a little uneasy, Ben looking at Sam. "Well," he said, "I'm here, ready to work. Where do I start?"

Knows Horses took him by the arm and led him to the corral.

Donna knew that Knows Horses had never laid her hands on Kyle. He was never allowed near her horses. Those horses were sacred to her. Only she and Beth worked to train them. They did it in harmony with the horse. When they trained a horse, he acted as if it was his pleasure to serve them. Having Ben with Beth all day, even in a stinky corral, would be a problem. Maybe it wouldn't work out.

Knows Horses had begun to speak to the horses. The ones she had been working with gathered around her, as if to not miss a word. Most people would use a lasso to rope a horse. This would upset the horse and make him harder to manage.

She asked Ben, "Do you know the language of the horse?"

"I don't, but I swear, I had a big buckskin that seemed to understand ever word I said. I bought him from a miner out from Silver City. I lost him when some claim jumpers robbed me." He wondered if this woman could have raised and trained his horse.

She watched as Ben gently touched the horses. He did not go around patting them or scratching behind their ears. He felt the horse with a smooth hand, and it settled with no fear.

Knows Horses said, "You start working this one. I will watch and show you if you do not understand what he wants."

I was working with some fine horseflesh, like the buckskin I had lost. I wanted to learn what this woman could teach me.

By the end of the day, I had been given many lessons. I saw early that nothing would be done with them unless Knows Horses approved.

As the day neared its end, I had gathered my horse and was preparing to go back to my cabin. Warrior Woman and Spring Flower came to tell Knows Horses they had a meal ready.

"We would like you to join us, Ben."

Ben washed and cleaned up the best he could. Spring Flower led him to a long table in the dining room. Beth and the others were beginning to gather round. For the first time that day, he thought about Donna, wondering why she did not eat with them.

It was lucky for him that he was sitting down the table from Beth— instead of across from her or beside her. He was afraid he might embarrass himself staring at her. The conversation was light at first, until they started talking horses. With the talk that went around the table, he felt he had not disappointed Knows Horses that day.

When Ben arrived at the cabin, Donna was there. She seemed to be a little upset with him. When he went inside, he saw that she had fixed a meal.

He did his best to apologize. "I did not know they would invite me to stay and share their meal," he explained, adding, "I surely did not expect you to be here cooking for me."

"Didn't you enjoy our meal last night? I only wanted to please you. I enjoyed last night so much. I thought you did too. I only wanted to be with you again." She pulled him to her and kissed him and began removing his clothing. Ben knew that she was taking control of him. This was the second night with her. He knew he did not have that effect on a woman.

He lay in Donna's arms, thinking of the beauty that he had seen today. He did not have a chance to talk to her. Donna had introduced him but moved him onto the rest of the family. It was as if she did not want him to become friends with Beth. He figured she was looking after her brother's future bride.

Donna knew she was running the risk of becoming pregnant. She needed to get her hands on that gold. She had to keep Ben away from Beth. She had seen how the young men in St. Louis had followed Beth—as if she were the only woman there. If Beth dismissed Ben, as she had the rest, things would work out. But she could not let her guard down.

After a few days of Knows Horses teaching Ben how to handle her horses, Beth joined the pair at the corral.

Knows Horses said, "These two horses are ready. Beth, take Ben with you. Start working them with the cattle.

Ben's heart jumped into his throat. He had only hoped to see her every now and then. Now he would spend the day working horses with her. He told himself not to stare and to try and talk to her like a human, instead of a goddess.

As she mounted, she began moving to the cattle. She did not bounce in the saddle. She moved with the horse as if they were one. Every move the horse made, it was as if she knew which way it would go. She gave the horse its rein; she was in control. Watching her, he was ashamed to mount. He knew that, next to her, he would look a fool.

They did not talk much on the way. When they made it to the pasture, Beth said, "We will teach the horses how to cut a steer from the herd and hold him."

"I am not sure what you mean."

"Watch me," Beth said. "And when you feel like you understand, pick out a steer and separate it from the herd."

Beth walked her horse to a steer. The horse seemed to know that this steer was the only one that it should focus on. She moved forward, and the steer turned to run. She encouraged the horse to keep up. As the steer tried to turn and return to the herd, she moved the horse left and then right. As fast as the steer could change directions, she would have the horse in front of it, and he would have to retreat. The steer could only go where the horse wanted it to go.

It was Ben's turn. It didn't look that hard. He eased his horse to the steer he had picked out. When the steer turned, Ben and his horse were on his tail. The steer cut to the left so fast Ben didn't have time to react. But his horse did. The horse and the steer went left. Ben went hard to the right.

It seemed as though Ben's face slid across every rough spot on that ground.

Beth was beside him, helping him up, looking at his bruised face. She took her scarf and gently washed his face with water from her canteen. Either she had hypnotized him or that was the gentlest touch a human could make. Maybe it was all in his mind. He had to quit being awestruck by her. He did not want to seem like a baby in her eyes.

"Beth, it may take me a while to learn to cut a steer. I had no idea that horse was going to turn that fast."

"You must move with the horse and watch the steer. If the steer turns, you must go in that direction."

"I am ready to try it again, but don't put your scarf up yet."

Beth laughed. It was the first time he had seen her actually laugh. Before it hi always been a smile.

Ben hit the ground again, but he landed a little better this time. He was hoping she would still baby him a little. As the day wore on, Ben got better and the two began to work as a team.

He was able to talk to her once he made himself understand—she was spoken for. She had this valley, and Kyle would be coming to claim her.

With the day's work accomplished, the two headed to the corrals. Along the way, Beth asked, "Would it be all right with you if we stop by Annie and Hamil's cabin? I haven't been able to come by much lately. We have had a lot of work going on. You haven't met them. Annie is my sister, and Hamil is her husband."

If it meant that Ben could spend a little more time with her, the stop would be fine. He'd heard the story of Hamil's sickness from Donna. It was a miracle he had pulled through. When the two of them rode up, Hamil was sitting in the swing under the porch.

Beth introduced Ben and gave a full report of him rooting up the ground. They all had a good laugh. It was not told in a way to insult Ben but to cheer Hamil, and he did enjoy the story. Ben spoke with him and found him easy to talk with. In fact, he was able to talk with him while glancing at Beth without getting tongue-tied. Annie had taken the care of her house back over. She wondered what had become of Donna.

Beth said, "I think she has moved back to the cabin." She did not imply that she was with Ben.

Hamil asked, "How much longer before the cattle drive?"

Beth said, "We will be leaving in a couple weeks."

"Do you think Zack will let me go this time?"

"If you keep improving, he would love to have you. But he will not take any chances if you are not back to normal."

After taking Beth home, Ben headed to the cabin. When he walked through the door, Donna started questioning him about the day's events.

"Did you see Beth today?"

"Yes," Ben told her. "We worked the new horses with the cattle."

He explained how the horse had taught him to hang on. He did not say that Beth and he had had a good day or that he felt like the two of them could become friends.

When he brought up the cattle drive that would be leaving before long, Donna quieted down and seemed to go into deep thought.

Over the next few days, Donna seemed to be in a slump. If Ben said something, she might answer or she might act as if she did not hear him. You never knew what her mood would be.

Ben continued to get better at cutting steers. He and Beth began moving them to the corrals—separating the cattle and getting them ready for the drive. It was not work, after he learned what it took to make Beth laugh. The pair had a good week working horses and cattle.

When he walked through the door at the end of the week, Donna was wearing a smile from ear to ear.

"How was your day?" Ben asked. "Something good happen? You look happy."

"I have a surprise for you," she told him. "When we go to Silver City, we can be married."

It felt like Ben had fallen off that horse again. He was having problems with his feelings about getting married. He honestly liked Donna. But he did not think he wanted to spend the rest of his life with her. The woman had mood swings, and he never knew what to expect.

The next evening, after working cattle, he asked Beth, "Do you mind if we go by to see Hamil? I need to talk to him."

"I have been wanting to go by and see Annie again," she replied.

Hamil was sitting in the swing. And since Ben had said he wanted to talk to him, Beth went in the house to sit with Annie.

"You seem a mite worried," Hamil noted. "What's on your mind?"

Ben explained the situation with Donna, saying, "I did not make any advances. She came to me. I do not want to hurt her. But I do not want to marry her either."

"What has Beth said about this?"

"I have not spoken about it to her. I would be too embarrassed. That is why I came to talk with you."

"Let me think about this for a few days," Hamil offered.

⸺⸺◈⸺◈ ◈⸺◈⸺⸺

A few days later, Beth and Ben stopped for lunch and to let the horses rest. He knew that he needed to talk with Beth about what had happened. Donna was her friend. He did not want to make Beth mad. She listened, without interrupting. When he finished, she looked at him real serious and then burst out laughing. Ben did not think it was funny.

In between laughs she said, "Pale Face, you are in one hell of a mess."

Ben could not help but laugh. When Beth laughed, it was contagious. You could not help but laugh with her.

Ben had expected her to tell him how stupid he had been. Sometimes he forgot that she was an educated woman.

"If you are not ready to marry, you should wait. Your heart will tell you when the time is right."

All was ready for the drive. The steers had been moved to the corral. The wagon was loaded with supplies. Hamil was to lead with the wagon, and Donna would ride with him. Beth and Ben would ride flanking the herd. Zack and Sam would ride drag.

At first, a few cattle had tried to get by the horses. Now they had given up and were staying with the bunch. Keeping the herd tight and moving made the trek a lot easier. With Beth on one side and Beth on the other, the pair worked back and forth, driving steers back to the bunch. When there was a cliff wall on one side of the cattle, Beth and he were able to ride together on the opposite side. As they were riding together, watching the dust rise from the herd, Beth asked, "What have you decided about Donna?"

Ben had not told Donna that he was not ready for marriage. He just did not know how to approach the subject.

Donna had been good to him, but why? Did she truly care? Or was she just lonely? This had happened so fast, and she had led from the first day. It felt as though she had everything preplanned.

"No," he finally said. "I have nothing. If your father had passed me by that day, I would be dead. From the first time I came into the valley, I've never wanted to leave. I would work for nothing just to stay here. But I think Donna wants more out of life."

Later, they stopped for the night in a meadow where the animals would have plenty to eat and drink. Ben was rubbing down the horse he had worked that evening. He saddled another one in case it was needed during the night.

Donna brought him a plate of food. She had kept her distance all day and had not spoken to him. So he was surprised when he saw her. She said, "I have to take care of my man."

Ben knew that he had to talk now. If he allowed this to go on, it would be much harder to stop. That was when he realized he did not want to marry.

"Donna, I must tell you, I think it is way too soon to be marrying," he began. "You want to go to San Francisco, and I am going back to the valley, if Zack will let me. We need to put this on hold. I know I am not ready."

Now Donna seemed to take that too easily, like she was not hurt. Rather, it seemed more like he had messed up her plans. After she seemed to think about what he had said for a while, she asked, "Are you in love with Beth?"

He knew that, if he wasn't, it was because she had never acted any way other than being friendly. He told her, "Beth is married to that valley, and Kyle told me he was returning for her."

She acted as if she believed him.

Donna lay in her bedroll thinking that all was lost. She had never realized that Beth was not looking for a husband. She had not cared for

Kyle, and he was waiting for them—thinking that Beth would come running to him when they arrived.

Her dreams of gaining control of that wealth were slipping away. She had actually begun to think it would not be so bad if she had to stay with Ben a while longer. He had proven to be a man who would be a good husband.

The next day, Ben got to talk with Beth a little. He told her what he had told Donna.

"When did you make the decision not to marry her?"

"I knew all along, but things were moving so fast I could not keep up with it. But when she brought me food last night, she was happy; an hour before, she was sullen. She can change so fast it does not make sense. I can't figure her out. But what it came down to is that I don't have the right feelings for her."

Over the next two days, things went well. Donna was friendly and said nothing else of marriage. Silver City had come in sight. Soon, the group would be able to pen the cattle and not have to babysit them. It was the first time that Ben would not come into town worried about anything. He had hopes that Beth would help him buy some clothes. What he had on were rags.

After they had delivered the cattle and horses, Zack took Beth, and they went to the bank. She told Ben that, after they had finished with the business end of the trip, they would have lunch and go shopping.

He had been window-shopping when he saw Donna come out of the hotel with her brother. He did not look to be in a very good mood. He gave her a push, yelling, "You are out of it. I'm taking over." He walked back inside.

When Donna saw Ben, she walked his way.

"I have lost everything," she told him, "all the plans with my brother, my marriage plans with you. I do not know what to do." She checked into the hotel and returned to her room. She wanted to be alone.

Over lunch with Zack and Beth, Ben spoke of what he had seen and heard.

They did not comment on what he told them.

Zack give him a sack of gold coins. "This is your pay for the two months' work you put in."

He held the gold in his hand and realized that this was the first money that he did not have to spend, other than to buy clothes. Any money he'd made before had to be used to replace supplies back at the claim.

"Are you coming back to the valley to keep working with us? You have been a good hand and have done a good job."

"I have been very happy there, and I was hoping you would ask me to stay. Now I can give Donna my money to help her until she can do for herself," he added. "I can wait about buying clothes."

"No," Zack told him. "Beth and I have already made arrangements to take care of her."

Beth and Ben picked out some clothes—or she did. What Ben picked out prompted comments on her part about how he would look like "a paleface dandy."

When people first met Beth, they had no idea that she would joke and laugh the way she did. The first time Ben saw her and how beautiful she was, he also noticed that her face was dirty and that she did not have on shoes. Most people's first response was to think this girl belonged on a shelf. She was a part of the valley, and that was the way Ben accepted her. He did not think she would be interested in a poor boy like him, and the two were able to become friends.

Beth did not want to be a St. Louis housewife to be shown off. She was just like Knows Horses. Give her a good horse and plenty room to ride. She loved her family and would fight to the death to protect them, and she would never leave the valley. Ben began to understand why she had rejected the young men back in St. Louis. They would not be able to live in her world, and she could not live in theirs.

As the two were walking back to the hotel, Ben asked, "What will become of Donna?"

"We bought her a ticket back to St. Louis. We gave her traveling money and a document to carry with her to the bank in St. Louis. We have an account there that will be changed into her name. We also gave her our St. Louis house. We do not need it any longer."

Ben felt so much better. He had felt responsible for her. But now he knew she could have a good life.

Early the next morning, Annie's and Ollie's tombstones were loaded onto the wagon, along with the other supplies. Zack and Sam would drive the wagon. Hamil, Beth, and Ben would ride horses on the journey back.

"This will probably be mine and Sam's last trip," Zack announced. "We are getting old; it hurts too bad making this trip every year. Beth will be taking over from now on."

This did not seem to come as a surprise to Beth or Hamil.

Later, Ben asked Beth, "Will Annie not be involved in any of the operations?"

"Annie is not interested in the care of the animals. She and Hamil want to spend their time camping and being alone. They work well together writing Hamil's novels."

CHAPTER THIRTY-SIX

We did not notice Kyle standing on the corner watching us leave. He had surrounded himself with his new friends. He pointed us out to them saying, "Digging out the ore is for laborers. Soon we will just ride into that valley and make a withdrawal with no interference. Those two old men will not be able to put up a fight. Y'all have already whipped Ben. He will probably run when he sees us. Hamil has been sick in the lungs and will be no problem. We will give them time to get home and settled down."

At camp that night, Sam said, "I ran into an old mining friend. He told me that Kyle has surrounded himself with some shady characters. We need to watch for them."

It seemed that Kyle had not gone to San Francisco as planned but had stayed in Silver City.

We took turns doing night watch, and during the day, one of us would ride drag about a mile back in case Kyle and his new friends were trying to catch up.

When Hamil was riding drag, I got to spend more time with Beth. She would ask questions about new breeds of cattle. The banker had told them the cattlemen were changing their stock. She asked what I thought of the changes.

I suggested that perhaps one breed might put on weight faster and be able to handle the weather here more easily. I noticed that Beth was bringing me into her confidence. She was looking to me to help her with her new position. I would need to always give her the best information that I could. I probably should start doing some research on the cattle. I did not know if Beth was really giving me a position. But I knew that these people had brought me in and treated me as family, and in this world, I might have to die for them.

I begin to think of the new threat that may be coming our way. After you entered the canyon, my cabin was about one mile in. I would be the first line of defense, and it would not do to get killed first thing. When we made camp that evening, I talked with Zack and Sam about a plan of defense starting with me. We needed to build a gate on the inside with some kind of alarm to go off when it was opened.

Sam had the idea that we could tie a piece of string to the trigger of a rifle. When they slid one of the poles one way or the other, the rifle would go off, warning us.

I also decided that the trail to my cabin needed to be changed and covered so it would not be noticed. If I heard the shot in time, I could light the fire and signal with my rifle. I would then head to Annie and Hamil's, making sure they could get to safety by going to the big cabin.

CHAPTER THIRTY-SEVEN

Moon looked back over his shoulder at the dead troopers and overturned wagons. This was the first time that he and his band had attacked the white man's army. He felt that it had been a huge mistake.

Big Ears was the leader of the band of fourteen warriors. They'd had success attacking the trappers and other Indian tribes. Big Ears felt that his medicine was powerful.

They had come upon the troopers while they were resting their horses. Both parties had been surprised, but the warriors had responded faster and killed all eight troopers. There were no supplies on the wagons. The eight dead men were on a return trip, having supplied the troops in the field. Big Ears had taken the guns and horses. Now Moon worried the army would be on their trail. If they returned home, they would lead the army to their families. He had not had enough time to talk Big Ears out of killing the troopers. It probably would have been of no use even if he had.

He was a half-breed and was not as important as the others. Only Little Cougar listened to him when he tried to warn them of the danger. He wanted to fight with his Indian brothers, but he remembered what his white father had told him. "You will never be able to stop the white man. They are too many and have too many resources. The army can follow you even when you have to stop to hunt food for your families. They will have wagon trains supplying the troops while you starve."

Little Cougar was his cousin and closest friend. He also wanted to keep the white man from taking the Indian's land, but he had listened to Moon. He understood the mistake they had made. Now all they could do was try to get Big Ears not to return to the tribe but to, instead, lead anyone who might follow away. They had asked Big Ears to make a trail leading into the mountains—a trail the army would follow. Once in the mountains, each brave would go his separate way.

Big Ears knew his medicine had been strong. He wanted a victory dance to show he was a powerful warrior. Now every warrior would want to follow him in battle. They had gained many horses and guns.

Little Cougar had been able to get enough warriors to listen, and together they talked Big Ears into going into the mountains. But he would not let them separate. Had his medicine not protected them? They might be able to kill more trappers. They would watch to see if the army would come looking for them.

That night, Moon and Little Cougar talked long of the mistake they had made. The rest were talking of how easy it had been to kill the troopers. With each tell, Big Ears become more arrogant and told of what he would do when the army came. He did not believe the cavalry would want to do battle with warriors that were led by him.

Moon was thinking how he and Little Cougar could abandon the others. He knew that, if they left, they would be looked at as cowards and deserters. He also knew a lot of innocent people would die because of what they had done. Little Cougar agreed with what Moon said but was at a loss to do anything that would not make it worse.

A week after they had killed the troopers, Big Ears sent a scout back to see if the army had come looking for their men. They would have been missed by now, and if the band was going to be tracked, the army would be on their trail.

Black Buffalo had stopped to water his horse in the stream when he heard the cavalry coming. He managed to get on his horse and ride upstream without being seen. They stopped where he had been to water their horses. He had been following the stream, but he knew they would see the dirty water he had stirred up when he was leaving.

The young lieutenant called the sergeant to him and asked what he made of the tracks leading up stream. Sergeant Barry was a hardened soldier who had been sent out to teach the lieutenant what he was up against. They were to bring the rest of the troops back to the fort unharmed. So far, the lieutenant had proved, like all the rest, that he was out to make a name for himself.

The lieutenant had made up his mind that Sergeant Barry was lazy—only wanting to go back where he could drink his fill of whiskey and chase the whores.

Sergeant Barry said, "If I were you, I would send a man back to ask the colonel to send more supplies and have them to meet us here. If you intend to send the scouts in to follow those tracks, take care. They could have been made to lure us into a trap. You did not want to return and resupply like I suggested. Now you intend to go into those mountains after the renegades. That will take at least a month, if we are lucky. Without being resupplied, we will run low in two days."

The lieutenant did intend to pursue and wipe out the renegades. He would not be this close and turn back now. He had the sergeant send three Kickapoo trackers to follow the trail. Two would track constantly; one would bring back word at regular intervals. The troopers were ordered to eat their meal for the day, as they may see action soon. One man was sent back to the fort for supplies and told to return to this camp and wait.

Black Buffalo slid his horse to a stop. As he dismounted, he was telling the others about the troops headed their way. He ran to one of the cavalry's fresh mounts, telling Big Ears, "There are too many to fight. We need to split up and go in different directions."

Big Ears would not have that. "No," he insisted. "We will take the army deeper in and find a good place to ambush the troopers." He intended to show his braves that his medicine was strong enough to protect them. He would let the army know that Big Ears was a warrior to avoid.

Moon made sure he had plenty of jerky and the best horse they had taken from the cavalry. He had a feeling they would make it, if only the horses could hold out. He instructed Little Cougar to do the same. He would need a shod horse and hope he did not come up lame.

Moon did not want to admit it, but he was afraid. There was no telling where this would lead them. They would need to avoid any contact with the cavalry. There would be enemy Indian bands to avoid, for they would be skirting Ute territory.

The lieutenant had the troops where the renegades had camped. According to the Kickapoo scout, they were only a couple hours ahead. He growled at the sergeant, "We should not have sent a man back for supplies. We will wrap this up tomorrow. You gave me false information, and the next time you do it, you will be busted down to Private Barry. The United States Army, when it is used properly, can handle any problem."

Sergeant Barry ordered his men, "Mount up and keep your eyes open. If we get into a skirmish, the Indians will try to pick me off first. If they get me, you will have to use your own heads. It will be up to you to get the lieutenant through."

Moon and Little Cougar were riding at the back of the warriors and could not see where Big Ears had taken them until it was too late. They had ridden down through the mouth of the canyon. After about five miles in, they saw it was a box canyon, with no way out. Instead of turning around and trying to get out, Big Ears had sent scouts out looking for a pass. It was getting late, and in the canyon, the sun would go down much earlier. When Big Ears realized his mistake, he made the decision to turn and go back out the way they had come in.

It was too late. The Kickapoo scouts fired on them. They were trapped.

They did not know it was only two scouts firing at them. If they had charged, the Kickapoo would have retreated.

Moon saw a place in the timber they could hole up and protect the horses. He and Little Cougar made a dash for it, and the rest followed. There was plenty of grass and water for the horses. They would need to eat and rest. Moon decided that tonight he would fight his own battle, or else he would die here. He would listen to Big Ears no longer. His plan was to let the troopers get to sleep, and he would charge their line.

Little Cougar was with him, and more was coming to say they would follow him. If they were to stay in the canyon, they would all face death.

Big Ears was against the plan. "The Great Spirit will tell me what to do."

"Did the Great Spirit tell you to massacre those troops?" asked Little Cougar.

Big Ears could not contain his anger and lashed out at the warrior who had embarrassed him. Warriors stepped up to Big Ears; words were not needed. Big Ears knew to step back.

One spoke up, "Now is the time to stay together. Some of us will die tonight, but the rest will escape."

Sergeant Barry had been informed of the renegades and the boxed canyon. He had the men hole up at the mouth of the canyon. They spread out and dug in for a fight. He told them, "The renegades will try to come out. It will be when the night is the darkest."

Before the moon came over the ridge, they came. They had walked the horses as close to the troop line as they dared. Some of the warriors had already mounted their horses. Little Cougar had listened to Moon and hung low on the side of his horse like Knows Horses had taught him long ago.

Most of the troops were dozing when the charge come. They were in a tight formation and coming fast. At the last minute, the warriors spread out and charged as if they intended to fight. The troops opened fire; three warriors hit the ground. The warriors were moving fast, jumping over the troops' line. The only other loss was Moon's horse. When he felt the horse jerk in pain, he knew it had been hit and kicked free. Little Cougar wanted to turn and pick him up but had been told no one would turn or stop. Those who died would not do so in vain.

Moon managed to grab the stirrup of a passing horse and, with long strides, ran with the horse, getting on the backside of the line. When he could keep up no longer, he turned loose of the stirrup. He knew he was close to the cavalry's horses. They would be picketed in grass close by, and probably no more than two men would be assigned to guard them. They thought the threat was in the box canyon. They would not believe the renegades would be able to escape.

Moon watched for any movement from a sentry. He knew that every movement of the horses would make it harder to tell sentry from horse. The best he could do was grab the first one he came to and hang on the side and hope for the best.

The first horse was a big buckskin like those Knows Horses had raised. It was saddled with officer's gear; it would belong to the lieutenant.

When the horse started moving, following the renegades' horses, with Moon hanging low, he was not noticed. At the outer edge, he sit up in the saddle and gave the horse free rein. He could hear the bullets pass close, but the big horse was able to get him to safety.

Through the night, each time he stopped to let the horse rest, he could hear the cavalry. They were not waiting for light to follow; they were going to stay as close as they could. They planned to ride the renegades into the ground. They would not stop until all were dead.

When Moon caught up with the others after the sun had come up, they had made camp and were cooking meat on the fire. Moon warned them the cavalry was following—that they could not stop.

Big Ears had taken control of the war party, saying his medicine had helped them again. Some seemed to be leaning in his direction for leadership. He had pointed out that, by following Moon, they had lost three men. He pointed at Moon and said he did not know if his medicine was still good after they had followed Moon.

Moon saw that it was no use arguing and led his horse to water and feed. They were blaming him now for the deaths, instead of giving him the credit for the escape. He rubbed down the big buckskin the way Knows Horses had taught him. He remembered the tale of Ollie bringing Zack to safety. Knows Horses had said Ollie had done it because he loved Zack. "Now let your horse love you," she had told him.

The more Moon worked with this horse, the more he believed he was a decedent of Ollie's. Many horses had been sold to the officers in the cavalry. They were the only ones that could afford the best.

Moon knew that it would not be long before the Kickapoo trackers would find them. He knew that his horse would be the only thing that would save him. He had spoken to Little Cougar about tending his horse, instead of listening to Big Ears brag. Little Cougar seemed to believe that Big Ears would have the medicine to get them out or destroy the enemy.

Sergeant Barry had asked the lieutenant to let the men stop, rest, and tend to their horses.

The lieutenant had brushed him off. "Our horses are in better shape than the renegades' and can ride as far as the Indian ponies can." He had lost his horse last night and intended to get him back. "The troops can eat hardtack and keep moving."

One of the soldiers asked the sergeant. "Is this all about a horse?" He'd had no sleep in twenty-four hours and nothing but hardtack to eat. His butt was sore, and he was sure the rest felt the same.

Sergeant Barry understood what the men were going through; all this was to help the lieutenant advance in rank. These men would never draw anything above a small monthly wage. He had already pushed his luck and would not risk his stripes. All he could do now was try to get the troops back to the fort alive.

One of the scouts had returned. Hearing what the scout reported, Sergeant Barry asked, "Why don't you let me and two men join the scouts and get ahead of the renegades? We could trap them between us and maybe put an end to this."

"Is this another one of your schemes? The renegades would spot you and be long gone. We have them now and will attack from the rear. If we kill enough, the rest will surrender. Have the men watch for my horse. I promise to buy the man who catches him a bottle of whiskey."

Moon was adjusting the girth on the big buckskin when the firing began. He saw what looked like four men go down with the first volley. As he swung into the saddle, he knew he had drawn their fire. It seemed as if every one was shooting at him. Limbs were falling from the trees all around him. One bullet tore through his left shoulder, and the big horse seemed to know it was time to leave. Moon hung on the best he could. He could feel the power of the horse, each stride seeming to get longer and longer. They had gotten out of firing range before Moon looked back. There were four braves following him; Little Cougar was not one of them.

The lieutenant was screaming at the sergeant for letting the brave get away with his horse. He promised the men that, when they returned, they would be retrained in marksmanship. There was nothing the sergeant could do or say. He had hoped to retrieve the horse so the lieutenant would give them time to rest before following farther. He had the men mount up and follow the renegades; he could hear their curses but did not blame them.

Moon waited for the rest to catch up. "What happened to Little Cougar?"

"We did not see him go down. If he has not been killed, he could be captured."

Big Ears rode to the front and began to lead the way. He was mad; he could see his fame slipping away. He would not be able to dance around the fire, letting the tribe see him in his glory. He would not be able to get any of the warriors to follow him again. He had left with fourteen; now they were only five. There would be much sorrow in their village.

When they stopped to water the horses again, Moon made plans to try and split from the few who remained. Without Little Cougar, he did not wish to follow Big Ears. He needed time to tend to his shoulder. The cavalry was dogging their trail and would not stop until everyone was dead. He could not ride much longer; his wound had festered, and the pain was more than he could stand.

When he approached Big Ears, he expected different than he got. Big Ears was glad to see him leave, blaming the problems on him. Moon knew that would be the way the story would be told. He managed to mount and ride upstream, hoping the army would follow the others and not miss his tracks for a while.

CHAPTER THIRTY-EIGHT

It was almost sundown when Moon stopped for the night. He had gathered herbs along the way that Spring Flower had shown him. After tending to the buckskin, he ground up the herbs. Now he had them ready, he would have to reopen his wounds, pushing out the infection. Then he packed it back with the herbs. While opening the wounds, he almost passed out; the pain was unbearable.

Sometime before daylight, drops of rain began to fall and awaken him. He had not felt it would rain and had not found shelter. The pain was not as bad; he would try to find a place to get out of the rain. If the rain continued, it would wash out any sign he had made. One hour later, he led the horse under an overhanging ledge and stripped the horse. If he was lucky, he would be able to rest a few days, letting his shoulder heal. Then he would head home. He realized he was intending to go home back to the valley, where he was never hungry or afraid.

Before dark, the Kickapoo scout returned. "We have found the renegades, but the buckskin is not among them."

The lieutenant had the sergeant send the scout back out. "Pick up that buckskin's tracks and do not return without the lieutenant's horse."

The Kickapoo scout's name was One Toe Missing. He had lost a toe as a child when his father's horse had stepped on it and cut it off. He had planned to return home before they'd found the dead troops. He had not seen his wife in three months. Now the lieutenant had sent him to track a horse. If he could find the tracks, that did not mean he would be able to retrieve the horse. He had seen this horse run and knew that there was not another horse in the cavalry that could match his speed or endurance.

One Toe Missing worked his way back to the stream; that was the last place he had seen the track. Once there, he headed upstream because that was the way he would have gone. There was no sign, but he would follow the stream, and maybe something would be found. No one could make it without leaving a sign somewhere. He came to a flat rock that the water had run over for thousands of years. This was where he would have left the stream. Following the stream took more time, and this warrior was in a hurry. He would leave without making a sign and hope the rocky surface would continue far enough that the tracker would give up and return.

The rain had washed away all tracks, but something disturbed One Toe Missing. The horse had not stepped on any plants that would stay bent over. Was this warrior that good? No. It was the horse. He had often thought he would steal the lieutenant's horse if he felt he could get away with it. There were pine trees ahead, and he would walk on the dead straw that would not leave any marks. Green brush would leave a bruised mark when stepped on. So far, he had seen no sign of the buckskin and the warrior who rode him. But this was the trail that he would have taken if he were hurt and trying to not be found.

He believed the warrior was hurt, looking for a place to stop and take care of his wound. But a man who was hurt would not be able to guide the horse so carefully. He had heard of a squaw that raised and trained horses. They were considered to be the best you could get; this buckskin had to be one of them. It was said that the squaw could talk to and understand horses. One Toe Missing decided that, if he could find and kill this warrior, he would take this horse. If he returned with the horse, they would only have another job for him. He would rather have the horse than a bottle of whiskey.

Moon had been able to move about without starting the wound bleeding and had managed to stake the buckskin in some good grass. With a few days' rest, he and the horse would be ready to travel. It would help if he could build a small fire and cook fresh meat, but the risk was too great. He knew someone would be following him; the lieutenant would not give up his horse so easily. The rain had washed out his tracks, but everyone knew that the Kickapoo were the best trackers and could follow a trail where there was no trail.

One Toe Missing had stayed with his logic—going where he would have gone were he the warrior with the stolen buckskin. He found a spot where someone had lain down before it had started raining. He had finally found a mistake. If the warrior was not hurt or if he had not rested his horse, there would have been no way to catch him. He was thinking of giving up and going home when he found a rock where someone had pounded and crushed herbs. The warrior was hurt and would not be too far from this spot.

He would leave his horse and walk. There had to be some sign somewhere; this brave was hurt and would not be able to think logically much longer.

One Toe Missing lifted his face into the wind and could smell nothing. He would continue up the side of the mountain. The wounded man would look for a location above, so he would be able to watch below. He would need a shelter; the nights would be cold. He would not build a fire; that would give away his position.

One Toe Missing spotted a shelf sticking out but was not in a position to see if anyone was under the overhang. He would have to wait till dark to move. From where he was to where he needed to be, he would have to cross in the open. If the warrior was watching, he would have no place for cover. Tonight would be the time to get a new position.

Moon woke, feeling much stronger. The herbs and rest had given him back a lot of strength. He would eat the last of his jerky. Then he would try to saddle up and head home. As he started to grab the saddle, a bullet tore through his chest, and he fell flat.

One Toe Missing ran to the spot where the warrior had hit the ground. The bullet had gone through his back and had probably hit his lung. He would not waste another bullet. He would claim the horse and be on his way. With any luck, he would be home in two days.

CHAPTER THIRTY-NINE

Spring Flower had decided to go and fix everyone coffee when the pain hit her in the back; it felt like it tore through her chest, and she hit the floor. The pain was so strong she could not breathe.

Zack was the first one to her and thought she was dead. She was not breathing. He moved back and let Knows Horses and Warrior Woman attend her.

When she was able to draw a breath, the pain felt like her chest would explode. She was not able to explain what she was feeling.

The wives tore her shirt off but could see nothing that would have caused such pain. While moving her to bed, she passed out and only took shallow breaths. When she was put in bed, they checked her pulse; the heart was beating regular. They washed her face and arms with cold water.

When she finally woke, she was determined to live. She knew what was wrong and started praying to the Great Spirit.

CHAPTER FORTY

Moon woke. The pain was so bad he only wanted to pass out again. Something moved, and he knew he was still in danger. He did not think he would die. If he did, it would be a comfort. He saw the scout pick up the saddle and head for the horse.

Apparently, the scout thought Moon was dead. He had not moved his rifle.

Moon knew that he had to muster the strength to take the rifle and kill the scout, or he would be left here, if not killed, with no way to travel. Now was the time. The scout believed him dead, and his back was turned to Moon. Without making a sound, Moon was able to aim and pull the trigger. The kick of the rifle hurt so bad he passed out again.

Moon did not know how long he had lain there, but the blood had crusted on his wounds. He had bled little, after losing so much blood when he was shot in the shoulder. He managed to get to his bag and get some of the herbs he had saved. Now came the bad part. He had to reopen the wounds and pack the herbs in the holes. The one in the back would be very hard to reach. After packing the wounds, he knew that the scout might be only wounded. But did not have the strength to check and passed out again.

The scout had been shot through the heart and had died instantly. The bullet had come out his chest and hit the saddle as he was putting it over the horse's back.

For two days, Spring Flower would wake and was able to have a little food. She was determined to regain her strength. She knew what had happened and was determined to live.

After two days, Moon was able to move very carefully. He had to find food. He had eaten the last of his supplies. He managed to find a few berries that the birds had missed; although he was still hungry, he felt a little strength return. If he could eat more of the berries today, maybe tomorrow he would have the strength to saddle his horse. He had to move before wild animals smelled the scout. With the blood that had been shed, they would come.

CHAPTER FORTY-ONE

Kyle had his men all meet him at the saloon in the hotel where he had been staying. It was time to put his plan in motion.

Kyle knew that, according to Donna, Beth and Knows Horses were the only ones who knew the whereabouts of the gold. He had six men, and he planned to sneak back into the valley. They would take up positions that he had mapped out while he was in the valley and watch for either of the women to go to the gold, allowing them to pinpoint where it was hidden. He believed that they would go to the hiding spot now and then, just to satisfy themselves that all that gold was safe.

Kyle had made sure that each man had enough supplies to last at least a month. When they came to the entrance to the valley, they passed it by and went to the small canyon that had held the cattle long ago. Of the six men with him, one was a Mexican who was good with the horses and would be left to tend them. Kyle and the other five would enter the valley on foot. They would fan out and go to spots that he had drawn on a crude map. All had been instructed to bring moccasins, so that they would leave no prints if possible. They were to watch and brush out tracks if they made any. When each man got to the spot where he would be able to watch the valley, he was to set up a camp where he could not be seen and make absolutely no fire. If any man saw one of the women go to a spot, he was to wait until night and then try to locate the spot and make sure the gold was there. As soon as one of them had located the gold, he was to report to Kyle.

Kyle knew the family would never tell him where the gold was, and all would fight to the death. He had heard the stories and did not want to tangle with them. It had been a stroke of luck that they had found the rifle set up for an alarm. The only sure way to find the gold was wait and watch.

⸻ ◈ ⸻

Beth and Ben had brought new colts into the corral to start their training. They now had a new barn to hold the colts in and a place to put the gear that they had accumulated. They had bought a new hay mower. It could be pulled behind two horses and would cut the hay and allow it to be stored for winter use. Knows Horses had ridden to the northern end to look at the grass she planned to have Ben cut soon. She also wanted to visit Sam. He had gotten to the point in life that his health meant more to her than more gold. He needed to come and spend the rest of his years where he would have company and care.

Knows Horses got off her horse and left him to graze while she went to visit Sam's camp. The horse had begun to stare at one spot up in the hills as if it had seen something. She went around in front of him and held his head while she looked into his eyes. From the way his eyes were pointed, she knew the spot. While she looked, she saw a brief flash of light. It had reflected off something briefly, and now it was gone. She gently raked her hand down his neck and went to see Sam.

He was sitting in the shade and was happy that he had company. Knows Horses spoke to him of the things they had been doing around home. When they seemed to run out of things to talk about, she told him that he was to pack his belongings. He would be moving to the cabin with them.

He knew that, when she spoke like she had, there was no arguing. He gathered his belongings and followed her out. He felt that, if he was not intruding on their lives, he would love to be closer to them.

She decided to walk. It was a beautiful day, and Sam was getting farther behind. She felt that they were far enough away that whoever was in the hills would not be able to hear their conversation. She asked if he had heard or seen anything that did not seem right.

Sam knew that, for her to ask that question, something was wrong. "A couple days ago, the burros acted as if they had seen something in the hills," he told her. "It must have been a big cat or maybe a wolf." That seemed strange because the last cat they had seen was three years ago. With more cabins being built, the cats had moved on. The last wolf they knew of they had killed. Knows Horses knew that what she and the horse had seen was real. Someone was out there watching Sam.

After they arrived home and had settled Sam in his new room, she called Warrior Woman outside and spoke of what she had seen.

◇━━━▩ ▩━━◇

Zane Potts had watched from his camp in the hills. The woman had ridden through the tall grass in no hurry. He had thought it would be nice when she came back and he found the gold to capture her and enjoy a few days with her. She was one fine-looking woman and she could help him pass the boring days. He may be able to persuade her to help him with the gold, and he would take her out of this place. He felt that this was going to be the time when she would lead him to the gold. She had taken the old man and his belongings with her when she left. He later decided that she may have moved him away so she could come back the next day and show him where it was hidden.

With the old man gone, he decided to ease down after dark. He would look around for any clue that he could find. He would not try during the daylight. Those horses knew that he was here, and if he moved, they might give away his position.

The moon was just coming over the ridge. It was a quarter moon; it would give him enough light to look around. He had found nothing to make him think that the gold was there, but she had moved the old man for some reason. He would get a good night sleep and be up early. He fully believed that she would return tomorrow, and this would soon be over.

He heard a thump but did not feel the pain until he tried to draw a breath. What was the matter with his throat? And why had he fallen? There was that woman in front of him pulling the string back on her bow. As he was drawing his last breath, he knew that she had cheated him out of his share.

Knows Horses and Warrior Woman had talked long the next morning. She had told Warrior Woman that the man had plenty of supplies—enough to last for a month or more. She believed that he was watching Sam to learn what he was doing with the gold. She said, "I am certain more are watching to see where the gold is hidden."

Knows Horses had buried the body so the buzzards would not be circling. There had to be more watching.

They decided that Ben should be informed about what they had found. Somehow the man had gotten in without tripping the alarm. With Spring Flower in bed, Zack and Sam would have to tend to her.

Knows Horses decided that they should ride more and pay close attention to the horses. If the horses had seen anything over time, they would look carefully when they returned to the location. While Ben was cutting hay, he would stop and rest the horses. He paid close attention to the direction the horses would stare or look at when he made a round. Not much got by animals that were raised in the wild.

Warrior Woman came to Knows Horses and said that Annie and Hamil had been lying under a tree below their cabin. She had stopped to talk, and while she spoke with them, the horse never stopped looking in one direction. It was the spot where they had killed the last wolf. She thought she had seen movement but did not stare at the spot. If anyone was there, she did not want to let the watcher know she had seen him.

Jeff Gilley hoped the young couple would come back the next day. Watching them made the day pass by a lot better. He had been hoping that someone would find the hidden gold before long. He had watched her. She was a very pretty thing and seemed to enjoy making love. He had already planned to keep her for himself after they found the gold. He had seen the cabin where they lived. If the shooting started, he was going there first to get rid of her husband and keep her from the others. The rest would have to find their own.

The moon was coming up, and with a little light, he felt like he could get close. He wanted to familiarize himself with the place and see how hard it was going to be to get in that cabin when the shooting started.

Wow that hurt. What in hell had popped him in the back?

Oh damn. What? Another one?

It hurt worse than anything he had ever felt. It was bad enough to put him on the ground. He could see the toe coming toward his face. The owner of the foot wore moccasins and was using it to turn his head up to look into her eyes. The woman's voice said, "The gold you look for is on the other end of the valley."

He knew where the stash was now but would not be able to tell anyone.

Ben felt the rest of the family should know what was going on and spoke about the matter to Knows Horses.

She had told him that the intruders were watching to see if she would lead them to the gold. If too many were out looking, they would know something was up. "We have killed two and believe there are likely at least four or more left," she told him. "If we can weaken them a little more, they may think that this is not worth the cost.

Kyle was hoping that his men were staying in position and not giving away their locations. He had watched Knows Horses ride down and bring the old man back. Since then, the only activity he had seen was Beth and that hand out working with those horses. He wanted to kill that hand; Beth was to be his. She was laughing and hanging a little too close to him. She had seemed to not enjoy his company as much, but she was probably just shy then. He should have killed the man back when they had found him starving.

Ben was riding the hay cutter today. Maybe he should go ahead and see if he could knock him off. If something did not happen soon, he would see how many of the men he could get when they were loading the hay.

That evening before dark, Knows Horses came to the hay field below Kyle's hiding spot. She seemed to be extra cautious, making sure that no one saw her. As he watched her, she disappeared into a crack in the wall. After about thirty minutes, she returned but did not have the brown sash around her waist that had been there when she had gone inside. He was so excited he wanted to run down and make sure, but he must remain cautious. When the moon came over the ridge, it was almost full and would light up the valley. He felt that, if he could get to the spot where she had disappeared, he could find the gold.

He worked his way down, and the horses were still on the other side. They had not spotted him and given his position away. Kyle eased into the crack; he was so excited that he almost missed the hole. To the right of where he stood was a shelf sticking out about two feet, and under it, recessed, was a hole about two feet wide. He believed that, once inside, he would be able to strike a match without giving off enough light that it could be seen. When he struck the match, he saw a candle sitting on the floor. She had used this when she had entered the cavern. It was here. What luck he had found it.

He thought maybe he should wait until the month was up and not let his men know he had found the stash. He could send them back for more supplies while he kelp watch. While they were gone, he would remove the gold. And when they all had grown tired of waiting, he could come back retrieve it and live like a king. Why should he share with them? He had already suspected that, if they did find it, they would have no use for him. His friends were like him, and double-crossing was part of the game.

When the candle flame lit the cavern, he could see there was a crack in the floor where she must have descended. There was a shelf, and he thought he could see bags lying on the shelf. He would have to get closer, and it looked like a tight squeeze. There to the right was a rock that he could step on and squeeze through. He positioned his leg to allow his foot to touch the rock and eased down through the crack.

Kyle was so excited. He was going to get some of the gold and rehide it while he was there.

When he took the weight off his arm and put all the weight on the rock, the rock came loose. He dropped so fast that he wedged in the crevice. His hands were wedged by his side and could not be of any use.

When Kyle had been in the hole over an hour, his legs started to go numb; he was wedged so tight the circulation was cut off. He had no way to let his men know where he was or the fix he was in. He did know of a place he would hide the gold when he got out. He had gotten Beth to go on a picnic one day. He had found a spot that he was sure the gold was in until he had gotten close enough to look. When he got out of this fix, he would move it there. The candle was about to go out, so he needed to hurry.

The next morning, Beth and Knows Horses were working with the horses, and Ben was cutting hay.

Warrior Woman came out, and Knows Horses told them that she had returned that morning and had seen that Kyle was stuck. He had stepped on the rock that she had knocked loose and replaced, making a trap for anyone who did not know about it. He had not known that she had returned and decided to let him die with the gold in sight.

Zack and Sam walked out to where they were. Zack said that they felt like they should be adding onto the barn. With the new mower, there was a lot of hay to be stored.

The women stopped talking. Knows Horses asked the men if they had consulted with Beth. She noted that Beth and Ben had already been thinking about the situation.

Zack asked why they kept Sam and himself around, if they were no good. When he had first met his wives and their tribe, they had not thought much of leaving the old people who were no longer useful to die.

Knows Horses and Warrior Woman went to Zack and said that he would always be useful.

"But what about me?" Sam asked.

Warrior Woman said, "You may have a reason to worry."

They all had a good laugh. And Beth explained that she and Ben had already decided to build more sheds. But, she added, they'd decided not to worry about it until all the hay was cut.

The next morning Knows Horses made her way to the crack in the wall. She went in and lit another candle. Kyle woke up when the candle lit the cavern. He said that he was glad to see her. He had seen her go in and not come out. When he had come inside to check on her, he had gotten stuck.

Knows Horses ask him if there was any way he thought she would be able to get him out.

Kyle told her she should return and bring help.

Knows Horses thought for a minute and said, "I cannot do that. If I bring back help, whoever I bring will know where the gold is." After a moment, she asked, "Did you get to see how much was there?"

"No," Kyle said, adding that, if she would help him to get out, he would share it with her.

Knows Horses asked, "Were you not going to share with Donna?"

Kyle said that he had wasted enough time with Donna, and she did not deserve a share. "And if we work it right, the other men won't get a share either," he added.

Knows Horses said that she might be able to get a couple of them to help get him out. "And then we will kill them," she concluded.

Kyle said that would work.

Knows Horses asked him to tell her where the other men were, and she would go for help.

Kyle seemed to not know who he was talking with. Most of the time he seemed to be in a daze and was not sure of what he was talking about. Maybe they would come with her. Then he would kill her. He told her where the others were hidden.

Knows Horses left and realized that he had given a fair description of where they were. She knew that most of the time he had been talking out of his head. But the two they had already killed were where he had said she would find them. He probably realized that giving up his men's location was his only hope.

Knows Horses talked with Warrior Woman and Ben and explained the information she had got and how they would handle the rest of the men. She would go to the spot where it was believed each would be watching. She would act as if she was hiding something, and Warrior Woman, after Knows Horses had left would watch and wait for him to make a move.

Knows Horses took the bag filled with sand. She hid it in some rocks under an overhang, and then left, acting as if she was trying to leave without being seen.

Odie Jackson wanted to run down and have a look the moment she was gone, but he knew that patience paid off. He would wait till he felt it was safe to go down and have a look. If the gold was there, he would let Kyle know. They would then get rid of everyone except that beautiful girl he had seen. If they wanted to know where it was hidden, that would be the deal.

He had uncovered the well-hidden bag of sand when the first arrow struck. Before he could get his breath back another one struck.

Billy Applegate knew that he was not going to let the rest know that he had found the gold. After this escapade had all been forgotten about, he would return for the stash. But two arrows put him down before he had a chance to look in the bag that the squaw had hidden.

One to go. Ben had already found where the intruders had kept the horses. He had taken great pleasure in killing the Mexican who had stabbed his friend to death. He had also found the horse they had stolen from him and brought the rest into the valley.

Knows Horses, Warrior Woman, Beth, and Ben rode the horses to the spot where it was believed the last one was hiding. Ben hollered as loudly as he could, "You are the only one left. These are your horses. Come on out, or we are coming in after you."

Slim Buckley cursed and started out. He had known all along that those horses would give away his location. He'd even thought of relocating after they had stared at him for half a day. But he had been told to stay in the same spot in case the others needed to speak with him.

When he walked out, he had a white flag around a stick and had left his guns where he had been hiding.

Warrior Woman raised her bow and said, "When you get to this arrow you need to run fast. But you will not make it. I want your scalp on my bow."

Slim tried to use his flag; he had surrendered. But seeing it was no use, he started walking and trying to figure a way to get back to his guns. When he arrived at the arrow, he knew that he could not run far. He pulled the arrow from the ground as he walked past, and with his next step, he felt the bullet come through his chest before he heard the sound.

Knows Horses had returned, and Kyle was weak but seemed to perk up a little when he saw her.

He asked if she had brought help.

"No," she said. "I killed them. But since you found the gold, I will let you live, and the gold is yours."

Kyle's last thoughts were not of making peace with his maker but of the fine houses and women he would have in San Francisco.

CHAPTER FORTY-TWO

Zack and Sam were sitting on the front porch when Zack saw a rider coming. He rang the bell, letting everyone know that someone was here. They were standing on the porch looking to see if they might know who it was.

Spring Flower got out of bed and came to the front porch. She started running toward the rider. Knows Horses cried out that it was Moon.

When Moon woke, he had no idea where he was. He could remember the big horse refusing to obey his commands. The pain in his chest reminded him of the bullet the Kickapoo tracker had put in him. He could remember killing the tracker and later climbing on the horse through excruciating pain. The horse seemed to have a predetermined destination.

Moon knew that he was lying in bed and could feel the presence of another person in the room. He could hear the shallow breathing, as if someone was sleeping. His first instinct was to reach out and see who was there. Someone must have found him and was watching over him. Could it be the cavalry nursing him back to health so they could hang him? He knew that it would not be long till daylight. He would wait, and if he had been captured, he would plan his escape without them knowing he had regained conscience.

Moon was awakened again by someone stirring in the room. After opening one eye and adjusting it to the morning light, he saw a familiar dream catcher hanging above his head. Spring Flower had made it for him when he was a child and had never taken it down. He knew that he had made it home. Or was this what the afterlife was like? Then he heard that soft voice speaking to the Great Spirit, asking to take her life and spare her son's.

Moon, in a very weak voice, said, "The Great Spirit has spared both of our lives."

Spring Flower turned and looked as if she were looking at a ghost. She sank to her knees and took his face in her hands, and with tears running down her cheeks, she embraced him. Moon was able to put his arms around her and hold her as he never had before. He did not know how long he had lain in that bed, but he knew she had never left his side.

The rest of the family, hearing the noise, began to fill the room. He could hear voices he had not heard in two years. The women were gathering around the bed, wanting to somehow make him more comfortable or feed him.

Then Moon saw the face of his father—the man he thought was the most powerful and kindest man on earth. But he had grown older. His long, black hair had begun to turn silver, and those powerful shoulders seemed to hang lower. The years were showing, and Moon knew most of it was from worry he had caused his father.

In the days that followed and as his strength returned, he explained what had happened and how he had tried to help his friends. But they had believed that Big Ears's medicine was strong enough to save them. Spring Flower told him that the rest had been rounded up and hung. Moon was glad that Little Cougar had been killed in battle instead of hanging.

He had spoken to Knows Horses of how the lieutenant's horse had taken charge and would not respond to his commands but on his own had brought him home.

After they had left Moon that morning, Knows Horses had taken the horse and given him her special treatment. She knew that this horse was Ollie's offspring. She had named him Mountain Breeze for the way he was able to move like the air traveled over the land. She had raised him after the last wolves had killed his mother. She had not wanted to sell him to the lieutenant, but Zack had said that perhaps someday some good would come from the sale.

In the weeks that followed, Moon regained a lot of his strength back and was helping with the light chores. He had formed a bond with Mountain Breeze and thought about how everything had worked to get him home safely. Soon, he would go in the mountains to speak to the Great Spirit.

CHAPTER FORTY-THREE

Beth and Ben had been riding and checking cattle and decided to stop and visit Annie and Hamil. Their teepee looked so comfortable under the large shade tree. Annie chose to cook outside over an open fire as her ancestors had. Hamil wanted to experience as much of the Indian way of life as was possible. The family had helped them to build a fine cabin, but if the weather was good, they would be camping.

After lunch, Ben lay in the grass under the shade and thought about how his life had changed since Zack and Sam had found him almost frozen and half-starved. Kyle Burks was dead, and Donna had been sent back to St. Louis. Ben knew that life was good here, and he had grown to love Beth more each day. He would have to speak to her, for he would not be able to face her much longer as just friends. Kyle had planned to marry her, although she had never spoke of him and seemed to not be concerned about his death. Ben had barely escaped marriage to Donna—a trap he felt she had set for him. Things were settling down now, and although Beth had never encouraged any man to come courting her, Ben knew he could not continue to face her each day as just friends.

Beth had helped Annie after lunch with the dishes. When finished, she got her horse and walked over to Ben and said, "Get up, Pale Face. We have work to do."

Ben loved the smile always on her face and to hear her voice. He loved everything about her. He wanted to talk to her and get his feelings out. If she turned him down, would he be able to leave the valley he loved so much? He felt that he would not be able to be this close to her and never hold her. Maybe he should wait for some kind of sign.

As they walked back to the cabin, Ben asked if they had explored the mountains to see what was there. Beth said she had always wanted to but was always too busy. When they arrived at the cabin, Spring Flower invited Ben to stay for supper. Ben was always eager to taste the meals these three women put on the table.

While they ate, the conversation was mainly about hay cutting and cattle. Then Beth spoke up and changed the subject. "We have lived here all this time, and no one has explored the mountains around us. The work is caught up for a while, and Ben and I are going to leave in the morning for a week or so and see what is there," she announced.

CHAPTER FORTY-FOUR

Ben could not believe his ears. He had always wanted to explore the mountains around this valley, but he'd never imagined it possible to have Beth with him as he did so.

The next morning, Ben was up extra early, preparing the things they would need for the trip. They would need extra blankets. The nights would be much colder at the higher elevations. He could not bare the thought of Beth needing something and him not be able to furnish it. He was so excited he decided he needed to drink another cup of coffee; he needed to think this through with a clear head. Ben knew he was a hired hand. The boss was taking him to help with the work, and he would need to remember that and quit thinking he was going on a camping trip with the love of his life. Beth had never changed her attitude from just being friendly. He could not let his mind go to wandering. He had too much to lose.

When Ben got to the cabin, he was surprised to see Beth was saddled, and packhorses were loaded. The rest of the family was still in bed. No one was out telling them to be careful and not to stay too long. Then he remembered that this valley, along with all the money, the horses, the cattle, and the gold had been put in Beth's hands.

The pair had worked their way up almost to the snow line by lunch, and it was funny how different things looked once you were there. At that elevation, they were able to look back across the entire valley. The beauty was overwhelming. They saw the cabin below with a large herd of cattle on one end and horses on the other. Ben allowed himself to think of a home there with Beth but was afraid to allow himself to think farther.

Beth found what they at first believed to be an animal trail. But the stones had been removed, and the trail was too wide; it was wide enough to drive a wagon through. Some of the limbs from the trees had grown out over the road, but you could clearly tell the trail had been made for a wagon.

Beth and Ben had followed the trail for about a mile when they found what had been a cabin. It had stone walls two feet thick and eight feet high. The roof had rotted away long ago. The doors had to have been massive by the size of the arched openings. This building had been planned out well before it was built; it was more of a fortress than a house. Around back was a fireplace for cooking, with stone arches that would have supported a roof to keep the rain or snow away from the oven.

Beth said, "We will camp here tonight. I will clean the oven. You get firewood." Beth had taken the small shovel from the pack and was scraping dirt from the floor beneath the oven when the shovel hit something that made a metallic sound. We both got down to dig with our hands and pulled out another piece of breastplate. Underneath was an animal skin wrapped around what looked to be saddlebags.

Beth carefully removed a book from the bags and opened the book. It was in fairly good shape but had to be handled carefully. "This is written in Spanish," Beth said. "We will have to take it to Hamil. He studied the Spanish language in college. He can tell us what it says."

Ben's world came tumbling down. What he had hoped would be a chance to be with Beth for a week or two was slipping away.

Beth must have seen the disappointment in his eyes, for she quickly said, "When we go back down."

While Beth cooked their meal, Ben lay out the blankets for their beds. Without thinking, he laid them close together. After he saw how close they were, he felt he should move his away from hers. But Beth was already handing him my plate.

After they had finished eating, Beth got in her bed without a thought. Ben was still sitting on his bed when she asked, "What do you think is in the book?"

Ben believed it was probably a journal of the gold that had been found.

Beth said, "I think it is love letters to someone that will never get to read them."

Beth had never mention the word *love* before. Was she one of those romantics who believed that the right man would come one day and sweep her off her feet? No. She just thought it was letters that a man away from home would write to his wife, planning to send them when he had a chance.

The pair talked late into the night of what was in the book and what they expected to find the next day.

The next two days were not eventful. They found nothing new, and Ben knew that Beth wanted to find out what was in the book.

"We should take the book and see what Hamil can make of it," he suggested. "I have been wondering what is in the book, and my mind has not been on exploring."

Beth agreed and seemed much happier to be going home.

Hamil and Annie were at the cabin when they returned. When Beth handed Hamil the book, he opened it to see what was inside. He began to move from chair to chair, as if he were looking for the perfect spot. The others realized he had found something very interesting and wanted to be in the perfect place. He would not move for several hours once he began.

When he realized Beth and Ben were waiting for some kind of information, he was embarrassed. He had not meant to ignore them but he had become so interested he had forgotten about them.

Hamil did not want to put the book down. He said that it was a journal and letters from Captain Mateo Abrego of the Spanish Army to his wife, Camila Abrego. Hamil said that he knew that we wanted information now, but he needed a few days to understand the document. He would write the story and let us know when we could read it ourselves.